D1630893

The Emperor's Rhinoceros

Thirteen Things 1

To Riva Dawar

The Emperor's Rhinoceros

Jack Trelawny

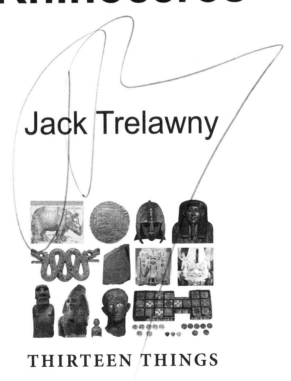

THIRTEEN THINGS

CAMPION BOOKS

Copyright © Jack Trelawny 2014

Jack Trelawny has asserted his right under the
Copyright, Designs and Patents Act, 1988,
to be identified as the author of this work.

All rights reserved.
No part of this publication may be reproduced, stored in a
retrieval system, or transmitted in any form or by any means,
electronic, mechanical, photocopying, recording, or otherwise,
without prior written permission of the author.

A catalogue record for this book
is available from the British Library

ISBN 978-1-906815-17-2

Front cover illustration by Jane Bennett

Other illustrations and images
sourced from Wikimedia Commons.
For image copyright enquiries,
contact Campion Books.

Printed and bound in the UK by
Berforts Information Press Ltd,
Gunnels Wood Road, Stevenage, Herts, SG1 2BH

First published in the UK in paperback 2014 by

CAMPION BOOKS
2 Lea Valley House, Stoney Bridge Drive,
Waltham Abbey, Essex EN9 3LY
United Kingdom

For my wife, Jane

Also for two charities:

Save the Rhino International

and

The British Museum

Save the Rhino supports many programmes protecting and conserving rhinos around the world. If your family or school would like to help with this protection and conservation work, a good place to start is their website:

www.savetherhino.org

The British Museum relies on funding from a wide range of sources to maintain its free service and there are many ways that you can donate to help ensure the display, care, and preservation of the collection for future generations. Visit their website to find out more:

www.britishmuseum.org

Donation to the two charities from book sales:-

I visit lots of schools (1,200 to date) to show children my books and share ideas about story planning and writing. 10% of the author royalty – from each copy of this book purchased in schools and elsewhere – will be donated (in equal shares) to the Save the Rhino and British Museum charities to help with their protection, conservation, preservation, and education work. Visit our website for updates:

www.jacktrelawny.com

THIRTEEN THINGS

Thirteen Things is a series of 13 adventure stories inspired by the joint British Museum and BBC project *A History of the World in 100 Objects*. The 13 objects or 'things' chosen for children by the museum and BBC are below. Thing 1 is 'Dürer's Rhinoceros'.

Dürer's Rhinoceros	Pieces of Eight	Sutton Hoo Helmet	Mummy of Hornedjitef
Double-Headed Serpent	Rosetta Stone	Benin Plaque	Tang Tomb Figures
Easter Island Statue	Statue of Ramesses II	Hoxne Pepper Pot	Head of Emperor Augustus	Royal Game of Ur

See the back sections of the book for more pictures, quizzes, activities, and web links. For colour images, maps, and other resources – including Jack's books, school assembly visits, and *My Story House* writing workshops – go to:

www.jacktrelawny.com

AUTHOR'S NOTE

Thing 1: Dürer's Rhinoceros

At the British Museum in London, there is a very old print made from a *woodcut* – an image carved on a block of wood with a knife and gouge.

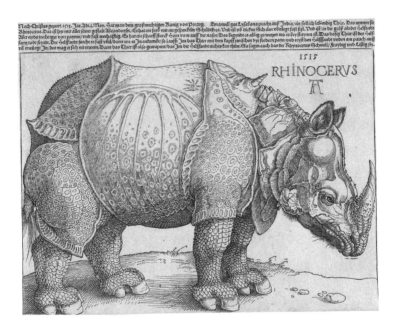

This woodcut print depicts an Indian rhinoceros called Ganda. It was made 500 years ago, in 1515, by a German artist called Albrecht Dürer.

Printing methods had recently been improved

and the picture was copied many times, so that lots of people could see it.

Ganda the rhinoceros was just like an animal described many centuries earlier, in the ancient stories of Rome, so he quickly became very famous.

The image of Ganda soon became known as 'Dürer's Rhinoceros'.

It appeared in numerous reference books for the next five hundred years.

Today, Ganda can be found everywhere, on all sorts of everyday items, such as mugs, T-shirts, and fridge-magnets.

The words written on the woodcut picture tell some of Ganda's story. The huge animal – a 'living gift' from a sultan to an emperor – was carried thousands of miles across the seas on a sailing ship.

In those days, the perilous journey from India to Portugal, around the southern cape of Africa, took four whole months.

The true story of Ganda's incredible journey can be found at the British Museum, and in many books and other records.

It inspired me to imagine this adventure...

CHAPTER 1

The Little Rhinoceros

The little rhinoceros chewed the sweet long grass as he roamed the vast northern plains of India.

He was still very young and small, so he made sure that he stayed close to his mother at all times.

He kept especially close to her on his first visit to the watering hole.

Peering cautiously from the edge into the muddy brown water, the little rhinoceros was very surprised to see his reflection staring straight back up at him.

It was only now that he saw a difference between himself and all the other rhinoceroses. The grown-ups each had a great big horn on the ends of their noses... where he had only a bump!

The little rhinoceros could not wait to grow older, because then he would have a magnificent horn on the end of his nose, just like all the other rhinoceroses.

However, he might not have been so keen to

grow older – and have a great big nose-horn – had he known there was a terrible danger to his kind in the world.

This threat came from ferocious hunters, who greatly prized rhinoceros horn; even more than jewels or gold.

The slightest scent of these vicious predators created terror in all the animals of the plains and hills and jungles of India.

These predators called themselves... 'humans'.

+ + +

Humans from the North, South, East, and West all desired the valuable rhinoceros horn.

Some carved it into dagger handles.

Many made it into cups, buttons, belt buckles, hair pins, or paperweights.

Others would grind the horn into powder and drink it in hot water as medicine; they believed it could cure fever, snake bites, and food poisoning.

For all these reasons and more, humans travelled to the plains in packs.

To hunt for the horn of the rhinoceros.

CHAPTER 2

Trap

One fine day, which had begun as happily as any other, the little rhinoceros followed behind his mother as she led the way along the path to the watering hole.

It was still early morning but the sun was already shining brightly in the sky.

Whoosh!

Crackle!

Snap!

Suddenly, the ground opened up and the little rhinoceros heard lots of awful cracking and snapping sounds as he saw his mother drop into a great big hole.

'Nrrrrrrrrrrrrrr!'

She instantly knew it was a trap and cried out, warning her youngster to run away.

But the little rhinoceros did not want to leave his mother; especially if she was in danger.

He ran to the edge of the trap-hole and looked

in, not at all sure what he should do.

It was soon clear that the little rhinoceros should have obeyed his mother's warning.

'Gaaahhhhhh!'

'Waaaahhhhhh!'

'Yaaaaahhhhhhh!'

In an instant, a pack of howling, growling, snarling humans had appeared from their hiding places.

They carried spears and clubs.

Bows and arrows.

And razor-sharp horn-cleavers.

CHAPTER 3

Big Bull Elephant

The little rhinoceros just knew these snarling animals meant to harm his mother as she lay helpless in the trap-hole.

He bravely put his nose to the ground and prepared to defend her.

'Snrrrttt!'

The little rhinoceros snorted.

Then charged straight at the hunting pack.

The humans scattered in all directions, swinging their clubs and stabbing at him with their spears as they jumped aside to avoid being trampled.

Ignoring the pain and the blood oozing from his wounds, the little rhinoceros turned to charge again.

'EEEOOOOOOAAAAHHHHHHHH!'

Suddenly, a gigantic bull elephant, with its human master sat astride its neck, trumpeted its arrival as it emerged from the long grass and stomped into the clearing at the watering hole.

The little rhinoceros was startled by the sheer size of the elephant and terrified by the noise it made.

Summoning all his courage, he charged at the enormous beast.

The elephant lowered its long, thick, curved, pointed tusks, and thundered towards the little rhinoceros, kicking up a cloud of dust and dirt as it gathered speed.

CACRASHHH!

The outcome was inevitable as the two charging animals came together.

The little rhinoceros was tossed into the air, spinning around and around like a ball of meat.

He landed heavily on the ground, badly winded.

As the little rhinoceros lay bruised, dazed, and gasping for breath, the leader of the humans growled an instruction.

'Lasso him!'

The hunting pack immediately fell on the little rhinoceros and beat him mercilessly with their clubs and slashed at him with their spears.

One of the pack quickly threw a strong rope around his neck; before retreating in haste to a safer distance.

Still fighting bravely, the little rhinoceros rolled over, stood up, and shook off the dust; making ready to charge again.

Facing his foe, the little rhinoceros could now see that the other end of the rope was swung securely around the neck of the big bull elephant.

'EEEOOOOOOAAAAHHHHHHHH!'

The elephant trumpeted again.

But it did not charge.

Instead, its human master pulled at its ear to turn it around.

As the elephant moved away from the watering hole, the rope tightened.

The little rhinoceros began to panic.

He didn't want to go; he wanted to stay to save his mother.

The brave little rhinoceros dug his toes into the earth and struggled valiantly as he resisted the pull of the rope.

But the noose became tighter and tighter around his neck and began to slowly strangle him as he fought to stand his ground.

He soon realised that he was no match for the

huge elephant as it began to march back into the long grass.

'Scrrrrrrrrrrr! Scrrrrrrrrrrrr!'

The little rhinoceros could hear his mother's screams as he was dragged away from her in the opposite direction.

It was probably best that he did not know why she was screaming.

CHAPTER 4

Buffalo Cart

'Mrrrrr. Mrrrrr. Mrrrrr.'

Still calling constantly for his mother, the little rhinoceros strained at the leash of rope as he was pulled on and on and on through the long grass.

He was very scared and anxious, because he had no idea where the humans and their enormous elephant were taking him.

+ + +

Some time later, they arrived at another clearing in the long grass.

A big cart was waiting at the start of a dirt track.

It was pulled by two water buffalo.

They stood patiently at the front, swishing flies with their tails.

Four of the human hunting pack walked up a ramp at the back of the cart and tugged on the rope to make the little rhinoceros get in.

He tried to resist at first, but two more of the

humans smacked him with sticks and prodded him with spears to make him go up the ramp.

The rope was then tied securely to a thick iron ring on the floor of the cart.

'Crrrrr. Crrrrrr. Crrrrrr'.

As the cart bumped away, the frightened little rhinoceros lay down on the hard wooden boards, and cried... and cried... and cried.

CHAPTER 5

Rajasthan

The cart rolled on for many long days and many long nights.

As the hunters left the plains, they entered the land of Rajasthan.

First they climbed steep hills covered in lush forests. Then they descended to follow a river.

The little rhinoceros could sense danger all around him.

Giant crocodiles lined the river banks, basking in the baking heat.

Snakes – vipers, cobras, pythons – slithered through the undergrowth and among the trees.

A huge male tiger had left his paw prints on the pathways.

As night fell, the tiger roared and chuffed in the near distance. The hunters nervously stoked the evening fire and kept their weapons close.

The next morning, after leaving the river valley, they began tracking along the edge of the Thar desert.

On and on they went, day after sweltering day, night after freezing night.

+ + +

After many such days and nights, the party reached a waterhole.

The little rhinoceros quenched his thirst.

The hunters took a long drink and filled their water pouches.

Then they turned their backs to the desert and headed south.

CHAPTER 6

Forbidden Fortress

One sweltering afternoon, an ancient fort appeared through the dusty haze on the horizon.

It sat high upon a large mound of barren rock.

This was the Forbidden Fortress; the lair and domain of the most feared and hated tyrant in all of India.

The little rhinoceros was taken through the huge gates of the fortress.

As they entered the courtyard, there was just one person waiting.

He was a giant of a man.

A terrifying warrior.

The giant warrior sat perfectly still on a jet-black horse.

His scowl was mean and menacing.

An aura of evil surrounded him.

This was the monstrous ruler of Rajasthan.

The infamous tyrant.

Raja Kadar.

CHAPTER 7

The Raja's Rhinoceros

Raja Kadar waved his hand, beckoning the leader of the hunters to come towards him.

The raja had made an agreement with the hunters. They would do a job for him: catch and deliver a young rhinoceros.

For this they would receive a double reward: they could keep the valuable horn from the mother; and collect one hundred silver coins for the youngster.

As the hunter approached, Raja Kadar threw a pouch of coins up into the air. The hunter caught the pouch, then bowed low as he handed the end of the leash to the raja.

The contract had been fulfilled.

The hunting pack turned and went out through the open gates of the fortress. As the evil raja watched them go, he curled his top lip and mumbled under his breath with satisfaction.

'Now I will have my princess!'

CHAPTER 8

A Cunning Plan

Raja Kadar wanted a beautiful young princess, Aisha of Gujarat, for his wife.

He had formulated a cunning plan.

The raja knew the princess loved animals. He would send the little rhinoceros as a gift to Aisha's father, the Sultan of Gujarat. With the gift, there would be a note. The note would say that poachers had killed the little rhino's mother, but he, Kadar, the great Raja of Rajasthan, had personally saved the young animal from certain death. The princess would think he was a hero who loved animals too, and she would agree to marry him.

As he thought about his forthcoming wedding, the raja smiled a crooked smile and clapped his hands. In an instant, a dozen or more servants had appeared from beyond the courtyard, all eager to do their master's bidding.

The little rhinoceros stood completely still, unsure as to what he should do.

CHAPTER 9

A Chance of Freedom

As the head servant approached, the raja let the end of the leash drop from his hand.

It was obvious that the servant was supposed to pick up the end of the rope; and he went down on one knee to do so.

But as soon as he saw the end of the leash hit the ground, the little rhinoceros knew he had been given a chance of freedom.

So he turned around and ran as fast as he could, straight towards the open gates of the Forbidden Fortress.

The raja bellowed at the top of his voice.

'STOP THAT RHINOCEROS!'

Two sleepy soldiers at the gates were shocked into action.

They quickly pulled the huge wooden barriers shut.

The little rhinoceros skidded to a halt and peered up at the great gates.

His heart sank as more soldiers ran to surround him.

With closed gates ahead, and humans behind, he could see there was no escape.

The raja now rode slowly forward on his big black horse.

His crooked smile had been replaced by an evil snarl.

He murmured menacingly to the head servant.

'Bring me my whipping stick.'

CHAPTER 10

Whipping Stick

The servant quickly fetched the whipping stick.

The stick was long, and knotted, and thick.

'Tie him to that post,' growled Raja Kadar.

Four servants pulled on the rope and tied the little rhinoceros to the post.

'I'll teach you to do as you're told and that you shouldn't try to escape,' snarled the raja, as he raised the whipping stick high above his head.

THWACK!

The stick came down hard.

'Ohrrrrr.'

The little rhinoceros yelped.

THWACK!

The stick came down hard again.

'Ohrrrrrrrrrr.'

The little rhinoceros yelped once more.

The beatings went on for days.

Every evening, just as the sun was disappearing over the horizon, the raja entered the courtyard with the whipping stick and an angry look on his face.

The little rhinoceros came to dread the setting sun.

'Crrrrrr. Crrrrrr. Crrrrrr'.

He cried himself to sleep each night, wondering whether this horrible nightmare was ever going to end.

CHAPTER 11

Tiny Tickbird

Eventually, the beatings stopped.

It appeared that the raja thought the little rhinoceros had been punished enough.

The wounds began to heal, and he gradually recovered.

But the little rhinoceros was still tied to the post with a short rope and he could not roll in the dust to stop the ticks biting him.

Then, one morning – just as the ticks were driving him mad with their biting, biting, biting – a tiny tickbird flew down and landed on the shoulder of the little rhinoceros.

The bird began removing all the annoying ticks with his beak.

The little rhinoceros was very glad to have such a helpful new friend.

He hoped the little bird would stay.

CHAPTER 12

Gujarat

The next morning, the little rhinoceros noticed frantic activity around the fort, especially in the courtyard.

Another long journey was about to begin.

The travelling party left the Forbidden Fortress as the sun rose above the horizon.

This time, there was no cart for the little rhinoceros to ride in.

He was once more tethered to the bull elephant with a leash of rope and forced to march behind the huge beast.

For many days they trudged along the mountain passes.

Then, late one evening, the little rhinoceros noticed the terrain changing as the forested mountains became grassy hills and farmers' fields.

They had entered the green and fertile land of Gujarat.

CHAPTER 13

Bustling City

On a particularly hot afternoon, the travelling party arrived at the edge of a high ridge.

In the distance, the little rhinoceros saw the biggest waterhole he had ever seen.

He could not know it, of course, but this was not a waterhole at all... it was the Arabian Sea.

As they advanced towards the coast, a city loomed ever larger on the horizon.

It was spread around the base of a big hill.

They arrived at the outskirts of the bustling city in the early evening.

The little rhinoceros had never seen anything like it.

There were thousands of humans all moving about noisily.

Some walked with heavy baskets balanced on their heads.

Others were buying and selling goods at the market.

Little humans chased each other around. They shouted and laughed happily as they played.

One little human held his mother's hand as she led him through the market.

The little rhinoceros cried inside as he thought fondly of his own mother.

He missed her so much.

CHAPTER 14

Palace of Jewels

As the little rhinoceros was led towards the centre of the city, it soon became clear where his captors were taking him.

Straight ahead, a beautiful palace stood at the top of the big hill.

They began climbing the slope towards the royal building.

As they approached, the little rhinoceros could see that the walls of the palace were sparkling and glinting, reflecting the light from the setting sun in a dazzling array of colours.

This was the Palace of Jewels.

The home of Muzaffar, the kind and gentle Sultan of Gujarat.

CHAPTER 15

The Sultan's Rhinoceros

The travelling party arrived, footsore and weary, at the gates of the palace.

A rider had been sent ahead with the raja's note, so the sultan's soldiers and servants were expecting the delivery of the living gift.

Without entering the palace, the leader of the travelling party handed the leash to an officer of the guard.

As the raja's men rode away, the little rhinoceros was led into the palace courtyard.

He was now the sultan's rhinoceros.

CHAPTER 16

Palace Zoo

The little rhinoceros was led across the courtyard and down a long tunnel at the back of the palace.

As he emerged from the tunnel, he could not believe his eyes.

There were hundreds of animals roaming the grounds of the palace.

Some of the most ferocious predators were fenced in for the safety of everyone, but all had plenty of space and food.

This was the Palace Zoo.

It stretched down the hill and into the distance as far as the eye could see.

The sultan loved animals and wanted his people to know all about them. He had collected lots and lots of animals for the zoo, and it was free for all the people to enter.

A man and a youth were waiting patiently.

CHAPTER 17

Zookeeper's Apprentice

The teenager was tall and dark and handsome.

'Hello, little rhinoceros. I am Akeem, the zookeeper's apprentice. This is my father, Rashid, who has given me the job of looking after you.'

Animals just know things, and the little rhinoceros could tell straight away that this quiet young man was gentle and kind to all creatures.

He was happy to follow as Akeem took the leash.

They set off down the slope and along the path through the zoo.

CHAPTER 18

New Home

As the little rhinoceros padded along, he became happier by the minute. He was comforted to see many animals that he recognised.

He saw tigers and panthers and wild boar.

There were peacocks and geese and waterhen.

Sambar deer browsed on berries.

Barking deer chewed the long grass.

A porcupine scurried along a track.

The little rhinoceros also saw lots of animals that he did not recognise.

A hippopotamus wallowed in mud.

Lions prowled their pen.

A giraffe plucked a leaf from the top of a tree with her long tongue and chewed it thoroughly before plucking another.

A huge snake slithered along the branch of a giant tree.

Young chimpanzees chased and wrestled each other in play.

Akeem stopped to watch three elephants being washed in a huge pool.

The little rhinoceros was scared of them at first, but he soon saw that they were very friendly; completely different from the big bull that had helped capture him.

Eventually, they came to a flat, grassy area, with a mud-wallow next to a large watering hole in one corner.

'This is your new home,' said Akeem. 'I hope you like it. We'll get you cleaned up and settled in. Then you can meet the princess.'

CHAPTER 19

Aisha And Akeem

The apprentice went to work, scrubbing and brushing the little rhinoceros to make him as clean and sweet-smelling as he had ever been.

While he worked, Akeem told the little rhinoceros a story.

'Princess Aisha and I have been friends ever since we were both tiny.

'My father is the zookeeper and her father is the sultan, so we should never have met.

'But we both love animals so much that we were allowed to play together in the zoo all the time when we were children.

'The princess helped with everything. She cleaned the pens and scrubbed the animals – and looked after them when they were sick – just like I did.

'But, as the princess grew older, she had to stop coming to the zoo, and now spends her time learning how to be a royal wife.

'She is very beautiful. They say she will soon be ready to marry.'

The little rhinoceros could tell that Akeem was sad that his friend, the princess, could no longer help him in the zoo.

He nuzzled his nose against the young man's legs in a gesture of affection.

Akeem smiled as he carried on scrubbing.

When the apprentice had finished, he sighed with satisfaction.

'There… you are ready.'

CHAPTER 20

Ganda The Brave

A message was sent to the palace.

A short while later, the princess was walking down the path towards them.

She was accompanied by her father and a large group of courtiers.

Akeem stepped forward, bowed low, and spoke in a soft, slow voice.

'Little rhinoceros, may I introduce you to His Royal Highness, the Sultan of Gujarat, and Her Royal Highness, Princess Aisha.'

The apprentice bowed again as he stepped backwards.

The sultan spoke, addressing the little rhinoceros in a loud voice for all present to hear.

'So, we finally have a one-horned rhinoceros from the northern plains for the Palace Zoo. Today is the day of your naming ceremony, little one. It was fortunate indeed that the Raja of Rajasthan saved you from the poachers and was thoughtful enough to send you here to live safely with us. By all accounts, you have been very courageous.'

The sultan then began clapping.

The assembled courtiers did the same.

The sultan held up his hand.

Everyone stopped clapping immediately and waited for the sultan to speak.

'Little rhinoceros, I hereby name you:

"Ganda the Brave".'

CHAPTER 21

Secret Glance

The courtiers clapped the sultan's words again.

Then they all turned to leave.

Akeem and Ganda watched them go.

Princess Aisha lingered a step behind all the others.

She stole a secret glance over her shoulder at Akeem and smiled at the handsome apprentice with great fondness in her eyes.

The young man sighed.

He loved the princess very much.

But they both knew they could never be together.

CHAPTER 22

Tikki the Loyal

Once the royal party had disappeared from sight, Akeem turned to the newly-named Ganda and saw that the tiny tickbird was standing on the back of the little rhinoceros, busily doing his job of removing ticks as usual.

'Well little bird,' he said, thoughtfully, 'they forgot to give you a name didn't they? I think you should have one too.

'So, I hereby name you:

"Tikki the Loyal".'

CHAPTER 23

The Mighty Rhinoceros

Time passed in Gujarat.

+ + +

Ganda grew from a little rhinoceros into a mighty rhinoceros; with a nose-horn to rival any he had seen at the watering hole.

His neck and legs were thick and strong.

His skin was like armour.

Everyone who saw him agreed... he was certainly an impressive animal to behold.

CHAPTER 24

A Royal Marriage Is Arranged

Meanwhile, Raja Kadar had been persistent in his pursuit of Princess Aisha.

He had sent other gifts and regular notes asking her father if she was ready to marry him.

But the sultan was a good man and he wanted his daughter to be happy.

He was not at all sure that she would want to marry this much older man, so he had been putting things off for as long as he could.

However, the sultan was also aware that Raja Kadar's power was growing by the day. Rajasthan had a huge army and an alliance by marriage might keep Gujarat and its people safe from attack.

Although Princess Aisha wanted to please her father, she certainly did not want to marry Raja Kadar.

She pleaded with him not to make her do it.

'Please father. He's so old. And I've heard such awful things about him.'

The sultan was sympathetic to his daughter's concerns, and continued to refuse the raja's requests as politely as he could.

But when the armies of Rajasthan invaded a neighbouring kingdom, the sultan was finally persuaded that he had to act.

He promised Raja Kadar that his daughter would marry him in one year's time.

On her sixteenth birthday.

CHAPTER 25

Spying Servant

Princess Aisha could not sleep on the night that her father told her of the marriage arrangements.

It was her fifteenth birthday, and she could not remember when she had had a worse day.

In just one year, on her sixteenth birthday, she would have to marry an old man who had a reputation as a despicable tyrant.

By the next morning, she just could not keep her love for Akeem secret a minute longer. She had to tell someone her feelings. She told her trusted maidservant all about it.

Unfortunately, another servant was listening at the door and overheard her careless talk.

This other servant was a spy, in the employ of the Raja of Rajasthan. Kadar had promised her jewels if she reported back to him on anything that concerned the princess.

The spying servant immediately sent a note to her evil master.

CHAPTER 26

Raging Raja

When Raja Kadar received the note from his spy, he was consumed with jealousy.

This soon turned into rage.

The raging raja kicked the walls and threw things across the room.

He made a vow to kill his young rival, Akeem the apprentice, at the very first opportunity.

His chance came sooner than he expected.

The very next day, he received an invitation to attend the Palace of Jewels for a grand feast.

This invitation suited Raja Kadar's evil plan perfectly.

He summoned his assassin, Hassan, and gave his instructions.

Hassan selected a vile of deadly poison, sharpened his stabbing dagger, gathered his other weapons… and made ready to travel with his master.

CHAPTER 27

The Sultan's Map

Raja Kadar and Hassan the assassin arrived at the Palace of Jewels.

After the grand feast, the Sultan of Gujarat showed his guests all the gifts he had received from the ambassador of a faraway country called Portugal.

One of the gifts was a map, showing the newly discovered sea route between Portugal and India, via the southern tip of Africa.

All present were fascinated as the sultan explained all the oceans and islands and faraway lands on the map.

CHAPTER 28

The Ambassador's Rhinoceros

'The King of Portugal is a powerful ruler, an emperor,' said the sultan. 'Some time ago, his sailors and warriors landed on one of our islands, just off the coast. They have showered us with presents. I hope you do not mind, Great Raja, but I offered a special gift in return; the rhinoceros you sent here. Their ambassador came to our zoo last week and expressed much wonder when he saw the animal. It would have been impolite not to offer him the rhinoceros as a gift.'

'I do not mind at all, Great Sultan,' said the raja. 'I will find another little orphan rhinoceros for your zoo.'

'You are very kind,' said the sultan. 'You may be interested to know that I have just learned that the ambassador plans to send the animal all the way back to Portugal, so that the emperor, King Manuel, can see it.'

Raja Kadar was *very* interested.

Because he knew that his young rival was involved in the care of the rhinoceros.

He used the discussion to try to gain some information about Akeem.

'Will your zookeeper be travelling with the animal?'

'Oh no, Rashid cannot be spared to take Ganda on the sea journey,' answered the sultan. 'His son, Akeem the apprentice, will be going instead. The boy and the animal are already at the port, waiting to set sail in the morning.'

This was something Raja Kadar did not want to hear.

He had assumed Rashid would travel to Portugal to look after and deliver the rhinoceros and it would therefore be easier to murder Akeem with his father gone.

This unexpected development had ruined the plan.

CHAPTER 29

Another Murderous Plan

Back in his room, the evil Raja Kadar could not get to sleep.

He knew he would need a change of strategy after speaking to the sultan at the grand feast.

He began to hatch another murderous plan.

After much thought, the raja summoned Hassan and issued his instructions.

In the middle of the night, under cover of darkness, the assassin gathered his weapons, donned his cloak, climbed over the wall of the Palace of Jewels… and made his way to the port.

CHAPTER 30

Galleon At Gujarat Port

The next morning, the Portuguese galleon was making ready to depart from the Port of Gujarat.

This was a spice ship. Akeem had learned that the Portuguese and other people in the West loved putting eastern spices on their food. He watched some men loading cinnamon and cloves.

The first mate shouted instructions as he supervised the loading of goods: 'Steady with that pepper, it's as valuable as gold!'

Other men were loading wooden barrels. The mate shouted again, this time much louder, as one of the barrels rolled along the deck. 'And be careful with that gunpowder; unless you want to blow us all out of the water!'

Captain Rodrigues, the master of the galleon, had insisted that Ganda was tied to a rail in a special pen in the hold, so that the rhinoceros could hardly move at all, let alone turn around.

There was not much straw to lie down on

and the only food they brought on board for the rhinoceros to eat was rice grain, which lay piled in a mound, just out of reach.

Akeem was concerned about Ganda but he could not do anything except speak softly and kindly to his friend as he fed him a handful of rice.

'The journey is one hundred and twenty days, Ganda. That's four whole months. I hope it will not be too uncomfortable for you being tied up for all that time.'

Ganda seemed to shrug as he nudged Akeem in the way that he always did to show his affection.

After he had tended to Ganda's needs, Akeem went up on deck. Everybody on board was dressed in European-style clothing. Except himself and a man who was talking quietly to the captain. The young apprentice had never seen the man before, but, from his black apparel, he looked as if he could be from Rajasthan. Akeem briefly wondered why the man was on board, but then gave it no further thought.

When everything was ready, the Portuguese ship set sail to lots of cheering and waving from the crowd of people gathered on the dock.

CHAPTER 31

Indian Ocean

On the first day of the voyage, Akeem began to feel very lonely. He could not understand what anyone was saying as they were speaking in a strange language.

One of the sailors seemed to notice this and began talking to Akeem in his own tongue.

'My name is Bartolomeu Dias, but my friends call me "Barto".'

'Someone who can speak to me!' said Akeem, showing his surprise and joy at the same time.

'Yes,' replied Barto, 'I can speak six languages. It is my job to translate for the captain.'

'Can you teach me some words so I can speak to the sailors?' asked Akeem.

'Of course,' answered Barto, with a kindly smile.

As well as beginning the language lessons, Barto taught Akeem lots of other things.

Akeem learned that they were heading for the

Island of Mozambique.

To reach it they had to sail across the Indian Ocean, to the east coast of Africa.

Akeem loved sailing on the ship.

He marvelled at the way the wind caught the sails and how it pushed the ship along through the water.

He loved the sound of the rigging, with all its creaking and cracking and groaning.

And he could listen for hours to the roar of the sea and the whistling of the wind.

Akeem watched the dolphins jumping in and out of the water as they escorted the ship.

He peered into the depths as the sharks circled.

Each morning, he looked up into the sky as the sun came over the horizon and watched the birds diving to catch their breakfast.

And each evening, as he went off to sleep in a hammock he had stretched across Ganda's pen, he tried to memorise everything that Barto had taught him.

CHAPTER 32

Equator

On and on the ship sailed.

It got hotter and hotter as the days got longer and longer.

'We are approaching the equator,' said Barto. 'We have an old tradition when crossing the line. Those who have never crossed it before must give a gift to the others on the ship. If you do not give a gift, you will be tied to a rope and dropped into the sea three times.'

'But I have nothing to give,' said Akeem, worried what hungry creatures might be in the sea that could bite him; or even eat him whole.

'Well I'm afraid you're going to get very wet then,' said Barto, with a concerned frown.

Akeem thought carefully for a long time.

'I know,' he said suddenly, 'I can give my wine ration. I haven't drunk any of it. I've been saving it because I don't like wine. I've been keeping it in Ganda's pen.'

'That will do nicely,' said Barto. 'You will certainly not get dropped in the sea if you give the crew your wine!'

A few days later, the ship crossed the equator.

It was even hotter than usual.

There was a big party, with everyone joining in, including the officers.

One sailor had refused to give a gift. He got very wet as the rest of the crew dropped him into the sea and hauled him back up on deck three times.

After his ordeal, the man was obviously exhausted, but otherwise unharmed.

Akeem was very relieved to see that the man had not been eaten by the sea-creatures.

CHAPTER 33

Island Of Mozambique

One morning, as the sun came over the horizon, there was a call from the top of the rigging.

'Land ahoy!'

The lookout had seen the Island of Mozambique. Here the ship would take on supplies for the next leg of the journey.

There was much activity as the crew made ready to dock in the port.

Akeem was allowed to leave the ship to look around the town.

He was sad that Ganda could not come with him but understood why. The mighty rhinoceros was far too big to be taken off the ship unless it was absolutely necessary.

Tikki alighted on Akeem's shoulder as he left and they went down the gangplank together.

The sun was shining and the waves gently lapped the shore as Akeem absorbed all the sights, sounds, and smells of Africa.

He immediately noticed that the people on the island had much darker skin than his own.

They were colourfully dressed in yellows and reds and greens.

Akeem enjoyed his walk on dry land and was very happy as he returned to the ship to feed Ganda.

But he would not have been so happy if he had known that Hassan had followed him down the gangplank and around the island.

The deadly assassin was watching Akeem's every move.

Waiting for an opportunity to strike.

CHAPTER 34

Cape Of Storms

The next stop on the journey was to be the island of Saint Helena.

'To get to the island, we will have to sail right down the east coast of Africa and around the Cape of Storms into the Atlantic Ocean,' said Barto.

'Sailing around the cape is very dangerous. There are jagged rocks everywhere and the wind blows so hard in gusts that sailors are swept overboard and never seen again.'

+ + +

Akeem had been dreading the passage around the Cape of Storms.

But nothing Barto told him about it could have prepared him for the actual reality.

The storms raged for days.

The ship pitched and rolled and yawed as the wind howled around them.

Thunder roared overhead.

The rain lashed down so heavily that Akeem thought he might drown whilst standing on the deck.

Eventually, the ship made it through the storms and passed around and beyond the cape into the calmer waters of the Atlantic Ocean.

CHAPTER 35

Island Of Saint Helena

The galleon headed northwest for the island of Saint Helena.

+ + +

On arriving at the island, they sailed into a small inlet, which served as a natural harbour.

There was no town, just a few storage huts strewn along a short pathway, which the Portuguese kept stocked with provisions for their ships.

There were no people on the island at all, just some goats and a few sheep introduced on previous visits.

The sailors rounded up some of the livestock and took the other supplies they required from the huts.

Freshwater streams provided clean water to fill the water barrels.

CHAPTER 36

North To The Azores

Underway once more, the ship headed north.

Akeem felt it getting hotter by the day as they approached the equator again.

There was another 'crossing the line' party.

That evening, Barto showed Akeem the map.

'We are now set on a course for the Azores. They are islands to the west of Portugal.'

+ + +

After many more days sailing, they arrived at the Azores and took on more provisions.

'We will now make use of the favourable Atlantic winds to take us east,' said Barto.

'It is the the final leg of our journey.

'Next destination... Portugal.'

CHAPTER 37

East To Lisbon

The Atlantic winds blew strongly and it was not long before the coast of Europe was in sight.

It had been four months since they had left India.

The ship arrived in the Port of Lisbon.

Akeem was surprised at the sheer number of other ships in the port.

Everything was strange and new to him. The sights and sounds and smells of this foreign land were very different from those he was familiar with back home.

As Ganda was unloaded from the ship, Akeem saw Barto talking to Captain Rodrigues.

His teacher and guide then passed on the captain's surprise instructions.

'Akeem, you are expected to ride the rhinoceros to the emperor's castle. Can you do it?'

CHAPTER 38

The Emperor's Castle

Akeem knew he was representing his country, so he complied with the instruction and rode the rhinoceros all the way to the castle of King Manuel, the Portuguese Emperor.

News of the arrival of the 'Beast from the East' had spread quickly.

Thousands of people lined the streets, waving banners and flags; and cheering them as they went along.

Akeem was worried that Ganda might be frightened by the crowds and the noise; but the rhinoceros seemed to be taking everything in his stride.

After quite some time, the castle was in sight.

With many tall towers and thick battlements, it was very grand and imposing.

Akeem guided Ganda through the huge gates.

CHAPTER 39

The Emperor's Rhinoceros

The emperor was waiting in person to greet them.

Akeem said the lines he had practised.

'Great Emperor, I bring you, Ganda, a mighty rhinoceros from India; a gift from the Great Sultan, Muzaffar of Gujarat.'

The emperor seemed delighted with his huge living gift from the East.

'I thank your Great Sultan for the gift. Can you tell me more about the animal?'

Akeem had learned a lot of the Portuguese language on his long journey, but he was still a beginner.

Luckily, Barto was there to translate difficult words as the young apprentice told the ruler all about the Indian one-horned rhinoceros.

The emperor seemed very interested in what Akeem had to say and he told the young apprentice he was especially impressed that he could ride on the animal's back.

'Thank you, Great Emperor', said Akeem, before he and Ganda went to their lodgings for a long sleep after their exhausting sea voyage.

CHAPTER 40

Dürer's Rhinoceros

News of Ganda's arrival in Lisbon spread very quickly across the countries of Europe.

Stories were told about him. Sketches were drawn. One such sketch reached a very famous artist as far away as Nuremberg in Germany.

His name was, Albrecht Dürer.

Herr Dürer drew the rhinoceros from the sketch. Then he carved the rhino picture on one side of a flat wooden board with a knife and gouge. It had to be back-to-front, a mirror-image. The result was a 'woodcut' that could be inked and pressed on paper to make copies of the picture that came out the right way round. The copies were called 'prints'.

There had been new printing inventions in Europe so that lots of copies could be made quickly and easily.

Albrecht Dürer had one of the new printing presses. He covered the cut side of the wood with black ink. Then he pressed the inky rhino picture on to some paper using the new printing machinery. Then he did the same again on another piece of paper. Then the same on another.

In this way, he made thousands of copies of his picture of Ganda and lots of people saw the image.

Herr Dürer had also put a written description above the picture, so that it too got printed and everybody could read it.

The words said: *A rhinoceros, brought from India to the great and powerful King Emanuel of Portugal at Lisbon, a live animal called a rhinoceros. His form is here represented. It has the colour of a speckled tortoise and it is covered with thick scales. It is like an elephant in size, but lower on its legs and almost invulnerable. It is also said that the rhinoceros is fast, lively and cunning.*

And so it was that, in a very short time, Ganda, the mighty one-horned rhinoceros from India, became known as 'Dürer's Rhinoceros'.

He was the most famous animal in all of Europe.

And – probably – the world.

CHAPTER 41

The Pope's Rhinoceros

All too quickly, it was time for Akeem to go home.

The same ship that had brought him to Portugal would now take him back to India. He said a tearful goodbye to Ganda on the evening before he was due to leave.

'Goodbye, my friend, I will remember you forever.'

Ganda nudged Akeem's legs with his head as he always did to show his affection.

However, later that same evening, Akeem got a surprise when he was summoned for one last audience with King Manuel.

'You have given good service to your sultan, and for that you should be extremely proud. But I would be very grateful if you could do an important job for me before you go home.'

'I will do the job if I can, Great Emperor,' said Akeem, very honoured to be asked.

'The King of Spain is building an empire in

the West, in the Americas,' said the emperor. 'He wishes to have the support of our Holy Father, the pope. He has just given the pope an elephant as a gift, in order to gain favour for his empire.'

Akeem paid close attention as King Manuel continued.

'I want the Holy Father's support for my empire in the East. Since the King of Spain has given the pope a magnificent living gift, I must do the same.'

Akeem nodded to show he was listening as the emperor continued.

'It would be very helpful to my plans if you could escort the rhinoceros to Rome, before you go home to India. I could give you one hundred silver coins for your services.'

'It will be my pleasure to do the job, Great Emperor,' said Akeem, overjoyed at having been given the chance to spend more time with Ganda.

He would have done the job for just his food and keep. But, of course, he was very happy that he would be paid as well. That much money was a small fortune to an apprentice zookeeper.

Captain Rodrigues made preparations to go across the Mediterranean Sea, to Rome, the ancient city that was home to the pope.

Akeem visited Ganda to tell him the news.

He brushed the rhino's hide as he talked.

After explaining to Ganda what would happen, he ended with: 'So now, my friend, you will soon become the pope's rhinoceros.'

The next morning, Ganda was loaded onto the ship.

Akeem noticed that the mysterious man in black had, once again, boarded with them.

But he gave it little thought as he was so happy that he was going to Rome with Ganda.

CHAPTER 42

Mediterranean Sea

The ship set sail from Lisbon and headed south.

For the next few days, as they sailed down the west coast of Portugal, Akeem spent a lot of time on the port side. He saw secluded harbours, busy fishing boats, and tiny, red-roofed houses dotted along the tops of the cliffs.

The woodcut print by Albrecht Dürer had been distributed everywhere; and news of Ganda – the mighty rhinoceros from India – had spread far and wide. People lined the cliffs and came out in boats to wave and cheer.

As the ship entered the Straits of Gibraltar, Barto showed Akeem a map. He pointed at different parts of the map as he explained.

'We are entering the Mediterranean Sea. Here, to the south, is the country of Morocco, on the continent of Africa. And here, to the north, is the country of Spain, on the continent of Europe. We are heading east, to here... Rome.'

Akeem soon noticed that the Mediterranean Sea was very tranquil compared to the Atlantic Ocean.

Sunny day followed sunny day as the ship sailed on.

Each fine morning, Akeem fed Ganda and cleaned the pen as usual before going up on deck.

The sea was calm, the sun was shining, and the young man was glad to be alive.

CHAPTER 43

A Terrible Storm

After the days of calm, a very unusual thing happened in the Mediterranean.

A strong wind began whirling and swirling around the ship.

The captain was not concerned at first.

But then the wind became a howling gale, which ripped and tore at the sails.

As the gale became a terrible storm, the captain gave orders to make for the nearest port.

Everyone on the ship began scurrying about, battening down the hatches and making ready for what was to come.

But one person on board was very pleased with this change in the weather.

Hassan the assassin.

For him, the worse the weather became, the better it was for his plan.

The killer knew that the chaos caused by a storm would be an ideal cover for a murder.

On a stormy night, he could kill Akeem and throw him overboard, pretending he fell, and nobody would ever know.

Alone in his dark cabin, the assassin smiled an evil smile as he slowly sharpened his stabbing dagger on a stone.

CHAPTER 44

Assassin!

The storm continued to rage into the night.

The ship lurched and rolled violently, making it difficult to stand.

Ganda was still tied to the rail in the hold and he shifted nervously with every clap of thunder.

Akeem was doing his best to comfort his friend in the pen.

'Steady, boy, steady,' he said, as he gently patted Ganda's shoulder.

A lantern was the only light. It swayed from side to side on its hook, creating shadows which danced and darted around the hold.

What was that?

Out of the corner of his eye, Akeem thought he noticed a shape moving in the shadows.

'Is anybody there?'

There was no reply.

He decided it was nothing.

But Ganda knew otherwise.

SWWSSHHH!

Suddenly, the mighty rhinoceros strained at his leash and swung his head at Akeem. It was just enough to throw the young man off his feet.

'Whaaat...?!' exclaimed Akeem as he fell.

But he soon saw why his friend had knocked him over.

Sqlch!

Hassan had brought the dagger down.

It was stuck in Ganda's shoulder.

A moment earlier, if Ganda had not acted, the instrument of death would have been in Akeem's back.

Ganda had saved Akeem's life.

'Grarghhh!'

The assassin growled with rage at missing his target.

He pulled the dagger from Ganda's shoulder, raised it high above his head and took a long stride towards Akeem. The evil look on his face made his intention clear.

At that moment, and just in time, Tikki dived down and pecked the assassin's ear.

'Owww!'

Hassan slashed at Tikki with the dagger.

But the little bird was far too quick for him and was already out of harm's way.

This distraction gave Akeem just enough time to grab a piece of wood to defend himself.

'Why would you want to harm me?' he shouted above the noise of the storm, as he held the wood in both hands in front of him.

Hassan snarled as the dagger's blood-stained blade glistened in the flickering lantern light. He was glad to tell his victim why he had to die.

'My master, Raja Kadar, says you must be killed. He discovered that Princess Aisha loves you. He wants to marry her and does not want a rival in the way. He will stop at nothing to have her. Once he has married his princess, he will kill her father, and take over as ruler of Gujarat.

'And, just so you know before you die, the raja hates all animals. He will roast and eat every last one of the animals in your precious zoo in a huge feast to celebrate his great victory.'

CHAPTER 45

Fighting For Right

Akeem began shaking with rage.

His *princess*.

His *sultan*.

His *country*.

And the *animals* at the zoo.

They were all in grave peril from Raja Kadar.

The young man quickly realised that he, Akeem the apprentice, must defeat this assassin and get home quickly to warn everyone of the danger.

Now Hassan made another move.

He slashed at Akeem with the dagger.

A gash wound opened on the boy's arm.

It oozed blood.

Akeem was much smaller than the assassin.

But he was fast and agile.

He stepped to the side and swung the wooden stick at the back of the assassin's head.

Clnk!

'Urgghhhh.'

Hassan groaned, dazed by the blow.

But the murderer was still standing.

WHHHHHSSSSSSSSSHHHHHHHH!

Just at that moment, a huge wave hit the ship.

Akeem was thrown to the floor.

Hassan staggered backwards.

Clnk!

His head clunked again, this time on a low beam.

He fell in a crumpled heap.

CRRSSHH!

The lantern now dropped from its hook into Ganda's pen, startling Akeem as the glass shattered.

The naked flame ignited the straw.

Fire!

Flickering flames instantly engulfed a large section of the hold.

Ganda strained at the leash that bound him to the boat.

Akeem knew the rhinoceros was a fine swimmer. But he would surely drown if he was tied to the sinking ship.

The young apprentice jumped to his feet, grabbed the dagger, and cut the rope.

BOOOOOM!

Suddenly, there was a huge explosion as the fire reached the gunpowder barrels.

Akeem was thrown across the hold like a rag doll.

Everything went dark inside his head.

He knew no more.

CHAPTER 46

Survivors

When Akeem regained consciousness and opened his eyes, he was staring at the morning sun.

He soon realised he was in the water.

Now he felt Ganda's massive form underneath his limp body, keeping him afloat.

Tikki was perched on Ganda's head.

The wreckage of the ship was strewn all around them. There were no signs of other survivors.

Akeem slowly recalled the events of the previous night.

'So, Ganda, I saved your life. And now you have saved mine. And Tikki helped too.'

'Yrrrrrrr.' Ganda agreed.

'Twtt. Twtt. Twtt.' So did Tikki.

Akeem now began to wonder how they were ever going to find a way to reach dry land.

That afternoon, he got his answer when he spotted a large merchant ship sailing towards them.

As the ship came closer, he could see it was an

Arabian dhow.

The Arab sailors threw Akeem a long rope and shouted from the deck.

'Tie it securely around the middle of the beast.'

Akeem did as instructed before swimming to the ship and climbing up the side to the deck.

He watched and thanked the men as they tied the other end of the rope to a sturdy rail at the stern of the ship.

One of the sailors cleaned and bandaged Akeem's knife wound.

Later in the day, after a short sleep, Akeem stood alone with his thoughts on the stern deck.

He smiled as he waved to Ganda.

It was a certainly a very strange sight to behold.

A ship pulling a rhinoceros!

CHAPTER 47

Do You Believe In Magic?

The master of the dhow was Captain Zafar.

He listened carefully as Akeem explained everything that had happened and what was going to happen unless he got home quickly to warn everyone of the impending danger.

The apprentice finished his story with words of deep concern: ' ...but even if we can find a ship to sail us home today, it will take more than four months before we arrive there. How can we save the princess? And the sultan? And my country? And all the animals in the zoo?'

The captain could see Akeem was very distressed.

The well-travelled and very experienced older man seemed to be considering what to say extremely carefully before speaking.

Then he asked a strange question.

'Do you believe in magic?'

CHAPTER 48

The Captain's Plan

'Well... ,' Akeem began, 'I have seen the tricks of the magicians at the bazaar... '

Captain Zafar interrupted him before he could continue.

'Because, if you do believe in magic, I know a man who may be able to help you.'

Akeem was intrigued by this mysterious information.

He nodded to show that he was eager to learn more.

The captain began explaining his plan.

He finished his explanation with the words:

'We need to get to Istanbul.'

CHAPTER 49

Corsica

Captain Zafar sailed his ship to a large harbour on the southern coast of the island of Corsica.

Akeem had learned that docking at a major port was the only way to get Ganda out of the sea and onto the ship.

After reaching the port, taking on provisions, and hoisting Ganda aboard, they set sail once more.

The ship headed east.

Towards the continent of Asia.

CHAPTER 50

Istanbul

After many days sailing, the dhow arrived at the Port of Istanbul.

'We must go to the Grand Bazaar immediately,' said Captain Zafar, as soon as they had disembarked.

With that, he set off in the direction of the city centre.

Akeem jumped on Ganda's back and they began to follow, with Tikki flying along just above them.

A captain, a youth, a bird, and a rhinoceros.

It was a strange procession, even for a place as exotic as Istanbul. Crowds of people stopped to stare as they went along.

After some time, they headed down a back street and stopped outside a little shop.

'Here it is,' said Captain Zafar.

Akeem looked above the shop. The sign read:

Mirkelam of Istanbul
Carpets and Antiques

Akeem was a little disappointed. He failed to see how a carpet and antique trader could help them save Princess Aisha.

And the sultan.

And Gujarat.

And all the animals in the zoo.

Lots of coloured beads on lots of strings hung down in the doorway of the shop.

Captain Zafar pushed the beads aside and entered.

Akeem slipped off Ganda's back, tied the rhinoceros to a post, and followed the captain through the beads.

CHAPTER 51

Mirkelam The Magician

A little, old man with a long, grey beard greeted them warmly as he hurried from the back of the shop.

'Ah, Captain! Welcome, welcome, welcome. Are you here for another present for your wife?'

'Good day to you, Mirkelam. I'm afraid that presents will have to wait for another time as we have very important other business here. This young man is Akeem, from the land of India. He has some great problems and I have told him that you may be able to help.'

'Ah, I see,' said Mirkelam. 'Well, as you know, Captain, I can only use magic in the cause of Good. I will need to know the whole story.'

With that, he beckoned them towards a little table surrounded by comfortable chairs. 'Come, sit here and tell me all.'

Akeem told Mirkelam the whole story. He told of the beautiful Princess Aisha, the evil Raja Kadar, the good Sultan Muzaffar, the long journey from India, the emperor's request, the terrible storm, Hassan the assassin, the shipwreck, the rescue by Captain Zafar, the invasion plan, and the threat to all the animals in the zoo.

'Hmmm,' said Mirkelam, obviously deep in thought after hearing Akeem's story, 'you do indeed have some rather large and pressing problems.'

'Can you help?' asked Captain Zafar, on Akeem's behalf.

'Your cause is Just and Right,' said Mirkelam. 'Which means I can use magic to help you. However, although I can give you the tools for the tasks ahead, you will have to use them wisely if you are to succeed.'

'Thank you,' said Akeem. 'I will do my best.'

'Come,' said Mirkelam, waving his hand to signal that they should follow him.

The old man took them deeper into the shop.

He stopped in front of a row of old, rolled carpets.

CHAPTER 52

Persian Carpets

'These are my Persians. Which one do you like?'

'It is very kind of you to show us your wares,' said Akeem. 'But we do not have much time. We must return to India as soon as possible to save the princess, and the sultan, and Gujarat... and all the animals in the zoo.'

'You have much to learn, young man,' said the wise old carpet trader. 'Please... just choose.'

Akeem glanced at Zafar.

The captain nodded.

The young apprentice looked along the row of frayed and faded old rugs.

A red one edged in gold caught his eye.

He pointed to it uncertainly, unsure whether his choice would please Mirkelam.

'That one?'

Mirkelam said nothing.

He simply smiled sagely, before turning and walking quickly towards the back of the shop, waving his arm to indicate they should follow him.

Akeem soon saw that the old man was heading for a tattered old curtain, which was hanging from a wooden rail.

He wondered what was beyond it.

Mirkelam pulled back the curtain to reveal a little room, which contained nothing but a single warped and splintered shelf along the back wall.

Akeem found it hard not to show his disappointment.

CHAPTER 53

Four Old Oil Lamps

On the shelf sat four dusty, old, oil lamps; with long, thin spouts. Engraved in large letters on each lamp was a different word. Akeem mumbled aloud as he read each word in turn.

'*Earth*.

'*Wind*.

'*Fire*.

'*Water*.'

Mirkelam also mumbled to himself quietly, apparently deep in thought as he stroked his long beard: 'Now, let me see, which one will we need?'

After much deliberation, the old man then selected one of the lamps and brought it down from the shelf.

Akeem was now even more confused. He failed to see how a frayed and faded carpet and a dusty, old, oil lamp could help in any way at all. He whispered his doubts to Captain Zafar.

'How can a carpet and an oil lamp help us?'

'Just wait and see, young man,' replied Mirkelam.

Akeem was a little embarrassed. How had the old man heard what he said?

Still holding the lamp, Mirkelam now hurried out of the room.

'Please bring the carpet,' he said, as he strode out of the door of the shop and into the street.

Akeem and Zafar, each holding one end of the carpet, followed Mirkelam out into the street.

'Strap the carpet to the beast and follow me,' said Mirkelam.

The strange little group – magician, apprentice, sea captain, tick bird, and rhinoceros – set off at a good pace.

They were heading east.

Akeem wondered where they were going.

Ganda wondered why a carpet had been strapped across his back.

CHAPTER 54

Jinjinn

They went to the outskirts of the city and climbed to a small wood at the top of a big hill.

'Stop here,' said Mirkelam, once they had reached a clearing in the middle of the trees. 'It is important that we are not seen.'

Akeem was intrigued. What was going to happen that people should not see?

'Please roll out the carpet on this flat patch of ground,' said Mirkelam.

Zafar and Akeem did as instructed.

'Now,' began Mirkelam, 'Akeem and the rhinoceros need to step onto the carpet. And the bird too, if he is travelling home with you?'

'Yes,' said Akeem, as he led Ganda towards the carpet, 'Tikki is coming too.'

'As quick as you can, please,' said Mirkelam.

'Is it a magic carpet?' asked Akeem, his eyes opening wide with excitement. He had grown up with stories of carpets that could fly.

'No,' said Mirkelam.

'Then how will it take us home?'

'Because this is a magic *lamp*,' answered Mirkelam, holding up the dusty, old object as he did so. 'Once you unleash the power within this lamp, the carpet will take you all home by the fastest and most direct route... through the sky.'

'But how does it wor...?' began Akeem.

'Take the lamp,' interrupted Mirkelam, before Akeem could finish his question.

Akeem took hold of the lamp in one hand.

'Now, when you are ready, rub the lamp gently with your fingers.'

Akeem did as he was told.

THNNDRRRR!

There was a loud noise, a bit like thunder, as a huge puff of smoke flew out of the lamp's spout.

The smoke began to form into a cloud. The cloud began to form into a shape. The shape wasn't quite a human. But it wasn't an animal either.

Akeem took a step backwards in surprise as the shape formed a head and a mouth and spoke in a very commanding voice.

'I AM JINJINN, THE GENIE OF THE WIND!'

CHAPTER 55

The First Wish

Akeem was amazed. He stood completely still, wondering what on earth he should do next.

'YOU HAVE THREE WISHES, YOUNG MASTER,' boomed Jinjinn. 'USE THEM WELL.'

Akeem looked at Mirkelam for guidance. Mirkelam opened his eyes wide and smiled warmly as he gestured with his hands to tell Akeem to go ahead and make a wish.

'I wish I could fly home on this carpet,' said Akeem. But he was not at all convinced that the carpet could fly at all, especially with a gigantic rhinoceros standing on it!

'YOUR FIRST WISH IS MY COMMAND,' said Jinjinn.

With that, the genie changed his shape to become more like a cloud again.

The cloud engulfed the apprentice, the bird, and the rhinoceros as it slowly sank towards the carpet.

To Akeem's surprise, it then began disappearing down through the carpet.

Once underneath, the cloud began to swirl.

Then it began to whirl.

As the cloud swirled and whirled, the carpet began to rise up from the ground.

It hovered at about head height.

'Now, say your destination,' shouted Mirkelam, above the howling wind.

'Gujarat City,' shouted Akeem.

SWSHHHHHHHH.

The carpet immediately rose higher and shot forwards as it set off in an easterly direction.

Akeem looked back and waved at Mirkelam and Captain Zafar.

'Goodbye... and thank you both.'

The magician and the captain both waved and smiled as they shouted together.

'Good luck.'

CHAPTER 56

The Journey Home

The carpet flew along deep valleys and over high mountains.

They saw deserts, forests, and plains.

They saw rivers, lakes, and seas.

Villages, towns, and cities sped by beneath them.

Akeem marvelled at how small everything seemed from such a great height.

+ + +

In just a day and a night, they were in sight of Gujarat.

CHAPTER 57

Aisha's Eyes

In the early morning, just as the sun was rising, the carpet flew over Gujarat towards the Palace of Jewels.

Jinjinn slowed his swirling and whirling.

As they made ready to land in the grounds of the zoo, the carpet gradually came to a halt and hovered in mid-air,

They were now right in front of Aisha's balcony.

The princess was on the balcony with her maid.

Aisha's eyes briefly met Akeem's.

She waved and smiled.

In that moment, he knew for certain that she loved him.

Jinjinn gently lowered the carpet to the ground.
SWSHHHHH.

As soon as the carpet was at ankle height, the genie swooshed out from under it and straight down the spout of the lamp.

The guards came running as Akeem stepped

off the carpet.

The teenager's voice was urgent and commanding.

'Take me to the sultan.'

CHAPTER 58

No Time To Lose

Akeem told his story.

In the middle of his account, he showed the scar from the attack by Hassan the assassin.

At the end he said: 'So you see, my Sultan, there is no time to lose. Raja Kadar might already be on his way.'

The sultan agreed.

'Thank you, Akeem, for bringing me this news. You left as a boy but have returned as a man. We need men like you for the battle ahead. Will you join us?'

'Of course,' said Akeem. 'I will do my duty.'

Rashid the zookeeper had been invited to attend the meeting. He was very proud of his son.

The sultan alerted his scouts.

The scouts returned to confirm that Raja Kadar's huge army was on the move.

An invasion force was heading straight for Gujarat.

CHAPTER 59

The Sultan's Army

In no time at all, the sultan's army was mustered and prepared for battle.

They set off towards the border with Rajasthan.

Sultan Muzaffar was at the head, riding on his magnificent silver-grey stallion.

Beside him rode Akeem, on Ganda the Brave.

Behind them came the elite mounted guards, each man on a strong war horse.

Then came the infantry; row upon row of marching men.

And so it was that the army of Gujarat was ready and waiting along the banks of a shallow river on the border between the two countries when the invading forces came over the horizon.

As the army of Rajasthan advanced, Akeem could see that Raja Kadar was riding at the front on a huge bull elephant.

Ganda knew from its smell that this was the same elephant that had helped capture him.

CHAPTER 60

Let The Battle Begin

Raja Kadar led his troops to the other bank of the river.

He shouted across with an offer.

'Great Sultan, why should we fight? Give me your daughter's hand in marriage; and we will be friends and allies.'

'Never!' replied the sultan.

The raja snarled.

'Then let the battle begin.'

CHAPTER 61

Tikki Taps The Lamp

Akeem was very courageous and prepared to fight to the death to defend his country.

But he could not see why so many men on both sides of the river should die because of the evil intentions of one tyrant.

He sat on Ganda's back, wondering what could be done.

Just at that moment, Tikki flew down and perched on the handle of the oil lamp, which was tied to the young man's waist.

The little bird began gently tapping on the lamp with his beak.

Akeem suddenly had a flash of inspiration.

'Of course, Tikki, of course!'

CHAPTER 62

The Second Wish

As the army of Rajasthan began to move towards the river, Akeem tore the lamp from its hanging cord and held it in front of him.

He rubbed it.

THNNDRRRR!

Once again there was a loud noise, like thunder, as a huge puff of smoke flew out of the lamp's spout.

The smoke began to form into a cloud.

The cloud began to form into a shape.

Jinjinn spoke in his very commanding voice.

'I AM JINJINN, THE GENIE OF THE WIND. WHAT IS YOUR SECOND WISH?'

'I wish to send the army of Rajastan home,' said Akeem, 'with no harm done to a single soldier on either side.'

'A NOBLE WISH INDEED,' boomed Jinjinn. 'SO SHALL IT BE.'

With that, the genie grew upwards... and he

grew sideways.

He grew and grew and grew, until he stretched along the whole length of the river between the two armies.

Jinjinn now started rolling over and over, churning up the water as he did so.

The raja's men stopped in their tracks.

A low murmur of fear and trepidation spread throughout their ranks.

CHAPTER 63

Tunnel Of Wind

Now the tunnel of wind rolled towards the army of Rajasthan.

'Attack!' shouted their leader.

Despite their fear, the men tried to advance.

But the force of the rolling tunnel of wind was far too powerful for mere mortals to withstand.

The cavalry were blown from their horses and the infantry were blown to the ground; weapons torn from their hands as they fell.

The soldiers had no choice. They began to ride and run back in the direction they had come, as fast as they could go; with Jinjinn, the Genie of the Wind, helping them along their way.

'HOORAAHHH!'

The men of Gujarat cheered in unison as they watched the invaders flee in a haze of dust and dirt.

When the dust had settled, a hush quickly descended.

All eyes were fixed on a strange sight on the

opposite side of the river.

The enormous bull elephant had been strong enough to withstand the rolling wind.

Raja Kadar had strapped himself to his mount and held on just long enough for the wind to pass by.

The evil raja was now alone on the riverbank, defiantly facing the entire army of Gujarat.

Akeem wondered what the sultan would do.

CHAPTER 64

Ganda's Revenge

Muzaffar was deep in thought.

He could order his men across the river to cut down the evil raja.

But the sultan was a kind and merciful man. He could see when his enemy was beaten.

'Go home, Raja Kadar, and do not return.'

'I'll go home today,' snarled the raja, 'but I *will* return!'

It was at that moment that Akeem felt Ganda surge forward underneath him.

The young man was thrown backwards.

Pmfff!

Akeem hit the ground, winded but otherwise unharmed.

He rolled over and jumped to his feet as the mighty rhinoceros charged down the slope towards the river.

'GANDA!'

But Ganda was not going to stop.

He had not been able to bear it a moment longer. The memory of his beatings at the hands of Raja Kadar had become too strong to ignore.

He charged across the river and up the slope on the other side.

'EEEOOOOOOAAAAHHHHHHHH!'

The great bull elephant trumpeted loudly... then lowered its long, curved, pointed tusks, and thundered towards the mighty rhinoceros, kicking up a cloud of dust and dirt as it gathered speed.

CACRASHHH!

Ganda was now fully grown. This time, the outcome was uncertain as the two massive, charging beasts came together.

SPLCK!

One of the elephant's tusks splintered and broke in two as Ganda crashed into it.

'EEEOOOOOOAAAAHHHHHHHH!'

The elephant trumpeted again as it began to topple over.

'Arggghhh!'

Kadar screamed in fear as the elephant fell.

'Nooooohhhhhhhh!'

He tried to jump clear but could not release

himself from the straps fast enough.

Akeem looked away as the elephant's huge body landed on the nasty villain, squashing the life out of him in one awful moment.

The elephant rolled over, rose to its feet and trumpeted again as it charged off back towards the hills of Rajasthan.

And so it was that Ganda the Brave had his revenge on the great bull elephant that had thrown him through the air and the nasty raja who had beaten him without mercy when he was small and defenceless.

CHAPTER 65

A Wonderful Royal Wedding

For his courage and service, Akeem was made 'Prince Protector of Gujarat'. Now that he was both a prince and a warrior hero, he could marry Aisha. The sultan said he would be proud to have Akeem as his son-in-law.

The plans for a Royal Wedding were made.

The marriage of Princess Aisha and Prince Akeem was a day of great rejoicing and celebration all over Gujarat.

Akeem arrived riding on Ganda, who was wearing his ceremonial rhinoceros robes. A special double saddle-box had been made for the occasion. The groom sat proudly in the front seat.

There was a lavish ceremony, with all the guests dressed up in bright colours.

This was followed by a huge wedding feast.

After the celebrations, Akeem and Aisha climbed onto Ganda's back and rode through the streets, with the crowds cheering and waving.

CHAPTER 66

The Third Wish

A few days after the wedding, in the afternoon, Akeem and Aisha were happily tending to the animals in the zoo, just as they had done when they were young children.

Akeem had been wondering what to do with the one wish that he had left.

He decided that, since he had now married Aisha, and was a Prince of Gujarat, there was nothing else he wanted; so he would give his Third Wish to his friend, Ganda the Brave.

+ + +

Next morning, when Akeem and Aisha visited the zoo to see Ganda and Tikki and all the other animals, they brought the lamp and the carpet with them.

Akeem rubbed the lamp.

THNNDRRRR!

Once again there was a loud noise, like thunder,

as a huge puff of smoke flew out of the lamp's spout.

The smoke began to form into a cloud.

The cloud began to form into a shape.

'Ohhh!' gasped Aisha; she had never seen a genie before.

Jinjinn spoke in his very commanding voice.

'I AM JINJINN, THE GENIE OF THE WIND. WHAT IS YOUR THIRD WISH?'

'Thank you, Great Genie, for all you have done,' said Akeem. 'I now have everything I have ever wanted. My Third Wish is that you grant my good friend, Ganda the Brave, his own greatest wish. But I'm afraid I do not know what it is that he desires most.'

Luckily, Jinjinn knew the innermost thoughts of people *and* animals. He spoke again.

'LEAD GANDA ONTO THE CARPET, PRINCE OF GUJARAT'.

Akeem did as he was told and beckoned Aisha to join them on the carpet.

Tikki alighted on Ganda's shoulder, chirping happily. He liked flying on the carpet.

A moment later, the genie became a swirling,

twirling wind once again and took off, carrying the carpet into the air as before.

Once airborne, it was clear that they were heading north.

Aisha spoke first.

'I wonder where he's taking us?'

CHAPTER 67

Back To The Plains

Jinjinn took them to the Plains.

Ganda saw they were heading straight for a very familiar watering hole.

'Mrrrrrrrrrrrrrrrrrrr!'

He called out as the carpet flew over the water.

Moments later, they were descending into a clearing.

'Hrrrrrrrrrrrrrrrrrrr!'

There was a distant call, which Ganda recognised immediately.

As the carpet touched the ground, Ganda's mother charged out from the trees, calling constantly to welcome him home. Thankfully, her nose-horn had grown back, just as it was before.

Ganda was overjoyed to see his mother again; and he shot off the carpet to greet her with a gentle nose rub and lots of little snorts and honks.

Akeem and Aisha had followed as fast as they could. The mighty rhinoceros paced back to nudge them both with his special gesture of affection for one last time.

The royal couple then stepped back onto the carpet to begin their journey home to the Palace of Jewels. Akeem waved a final farewell as the carpet rose into the air.

'Goodbye Ganda. Goodbye Tikki. And thank you for everything, my brave and loyal friends.'

THE END

NEXT

Story 2, Quizzes, Facts, See and Do

For this first story in the *Thirteen Things* series, *The Emperor's Rhinoceros*, we travelled back in time to Asia, Africa, and Europe in the year 1515.

After reading this book, you may like to read the next story in the series, *8 Pieces of Eight*, which transports us back to Africa and South America in the year 1596.

In the meantime, turn the pages to find out more about rhinoceroses and the 13 objects that have provided the inspiration for the *Thirteen Things* series, as well as some quizzes and other things to see and do...

- Quiz 1: *The Emperor's Rhinoceros*
- Fun Facts: About Rhinoceroses
- Quiz 2: About Rhinoceroses
- Save the Rhino International
- Ganda's Journey - Map: Real vs Pretend
- Story Detectives: At the British Museum
- Jack Trelawny: School Author Visitor
- Quiz Answers

QUIZ 1

The Emperor's Rhinoceros

This quiz is based on the first story in the *Thirteen Things* series, *The Emperor's Rhinoceros*. Answers at the back of the book. See www.jacktrelawny.com to print quizzes.

1) Where was Ganda born?
    A)   Africa
    B)   Sumatra
    C)   Java
    D)   India

2) How many horns will Ganda have when he grows up?
    A)   Two
    B)   One
    C)   Four
    D)   Three

3) Which type of animal helps the humans capture Ganda?
    A)   Dog
    B)   Horse
    C)   Elephant
    D)   Tiger

4) Where is the Forbidden Fortress?
    A)   Rajasthan
    B)   Gujarat
    C)   Mozambique
    D)   Lisbon

5) How long does the India to Portugal sea-journey take?
- A)   100 days
- B)   110 days
- C)   120 days
- D)   130 days

6) What is the Portuguese Emperor called?
- A)   King Rodrigues
- B)   King Barto
- C)   King Muzaffar
- D)   King Manuel

7) What type of ship is sailed by Captain Zafar?
- A)   Dhow
- B)   Longship
- C)   Galleon
- D)   Trawler

8) Where is Mirkelam's shop?
- A)   Lisbon
- B)   Saint Helena
- C)   Corsica
- D)   Istanbul

9) How many oil lamps are on the shelf in the shop?
- A)   Five
- B)   Three
- C)   Four
- D)   Two

10) How many Wishes does Jinjinn allow Akeem?
- A)   Five
- B)   Three
- C)   Four
- D)   Two

FUN FACTS

About Rhinoceroses

Much of the information in this section is sourced from web pages at this link:

www.savetherhino.org/rhino_info/for_kids

Schools and families may like to visit this website to find out much more about rhinoceroses and to see what can be done to help save them from extinction.

Author's Note: The facts and figures about rhinoceroses in different books and websites I have looked at vary from one source to the next. For example, one source may say that there are only 90 of a particular type of rhinoceros left alive, whilst another source will estimate the number at 200. This may be because it is sometimes difficult to be exact, especially when talking about shy animals that live in jungles and are hard to find, let alone count. So you may like to do your own finding out to compare what different sources say about numbers, sizes, and so on.

1. There are five different species of living rhinoceros as well as extinct species. One extinct species is the woolly rhinoceros. Three of the living species, Indian rhinoceros, Javan rhinoceros, and Sumatran rhinoceros, are from southern Asia. The other two living species, black rhinoceros and white rhinoceros, are from Africa.

2. The name rhinoceros means 'nose horn' and is often shortened to 'rhino'. It comes from the Greek words rhino (nose) and ceros (horn). Both African species – and the Sumatran rhinoceros – have two horns, while the Indian and Javan rhinoceros have a single horn.

3. The white rhinoceros is the second largest land mammal. The white rhino is the largest rhino species. It can weigh over 4,000 kg and is the largest land mammal after the elephant. (Note: elephants can grow to be as much as 7,000 kg.)

4. Rhinos can grow to over 1.8 m tall and more than 3.4 m in length.

5. Three of the five rhinoceros species are listed as being 'Critically Endangered'. The black rhinoceros, Javan rhinoceros, and Sumatran rhinoceros are all 'Critically Endangered'; which means they have a 50% chance of becoming extinct in three generations.

6. Rhinoceroses have thick, sensitive skin. Rhino skin may be thick, but it can be quite sensitive to sunburn and insect bites, which is why they like to wallow in mud so much. When the mud dries, it acts as protection from the sunburn and insects.

7. Relative to their large body size, rhinoceroses have small brains. But they are quite intelligent.

8. Rhinoceros horn is made from a protein called keratin, the same substance that fingernails and hair are made of. The rhino's horn is not bone and is not attached to its skull; it is also not hollow like elephant tusks. It is actually a dense mass of hairs that continues to grow throughout the animal's lifetime, just like our own hair and nails. The horn averages about 51 cm in length on the black rhino. However, the longest known on this species was 145 cm. That's longer than the average height (142 cm) of a ten-year-old human child!

9. Some rhinos use their teeth – not their horns – for defence. When a greater one-horned rhinoceros is threatened, it slashes and gouges with its long, sharp incisors and the canine teeth of its lower jaw.

10. Rhinos are herbivores (plant eaters). They have to eat a lot to fill their large bodies.

11. A group of rhinos is called a 'crash'. Many rhinos live a solitary life, which means they are often alone. However, when there's a group, we can say, 'there's a *crash* of rhinos'!

12. Despite their names, both the 'white' and 'black' rhinoceros are actually grey. The white rhino's name may be taken from the Afrikaans word, 'wijd' (pronounced something like 'vait'), which means 'wide' and describes its mouth. Early English settlers in South Africa could have misinterpreted 'wijd' for 'white'. Black rhinos possibly got their name from the dark wet mud in their wallows that made them appear black. Both species are basically grey in colour.

13. The closest living rhino 'relatives' are tapirs, horses, and zebras. All rhinos have three toes, with distinct toenails. They are part of a group of mammals called 'odd-toed ungulates'.

14. Rhinos are speed machines. The fastest rhinos can run at 45 km/h. The fastest human, Usain Bolt, can reach a top speed of 44.72 km/h for a few seconds. So, unless you can run like Mr Bolt over a long distance, it might be best to climb a tree if a rhino is chasing you!

15. Rhino pregnancies last a long time. Females are pregnant for 15-16 months. Mother rhinos are very nurturing. The young stay with their mothers until they are approximately 3 years old.

16. Rhinos have poor eyesight, but very well-developed senses of smell and hearing. A rhino has trouble detecting a person standing 30 m away with its eyes if the individual remains still. However, if the person makes the faintest sound, or the rhino is able to smell the person, it will easily detect them, even at much greater distances. The 'olfactory' (sense of smell) portion is the largest area of the rhino's brain.

17. African rhinos are a good 'home' for oxpeckers. The oxpecker eats ticks and other insects that it finds on the rhino, and creates a commotion when it senses danger. This helps alert the rhino.

18. Rhino's communicate by doing a poo! Rhinos use piles of dung to leave 'messages' for other rhinos, such as 'this is my territory'. Each rhino's smell is unique and identifies its owner. The smell can also indicate to one rhino whether another is young/old or male/female.

19. Rhinos are over 50 million years old. They haven't changed much since prehistoric times. Some of the first rhinos didn't have horns. As well as Africa and Asia, they once roamed throughout North America and Europe. Rhino fossils have never been found in South America or Australia.

20. Woolly rhinos evolved to survive the Ice Age cold. When the earth became much colder, woolly rhinos grew thick, shaggy coats to keep them warm. They were hunted by early humans and are depicted in cave paintings dating back more than 30,000 years ago. The Sumatran rhino is the closest living relative of the ancient extinct woolly rhino. Unlike most other rhinos, the hide of the Sumatran rhino, grey-brown in colour, is covered with patches of short, dark, stiff hair.

21. Lips for feeding. The black rhino has a hooked lip which allows it to feed on trees and shrubs. The white rhino has a long, flat, upper lip which is perfect for grazing on grasses. The upper lips of the three Asian rhino species allow these animals to browse vegetation in tropical forest habitats.

22. *The Javan rhino is the world's rarest land mammal.* There are no Javan rhinos living in zoos and it is thought that less than 50 individuals survive in the wild.

23. Not all rhinos are solitary creatures. White rhinos commonly live in extended family groups, particularly females and their calves, and can sometimes be seen in large numbers. The largest groups, however, appear to be those of greater one-horned rhinos in India's Kaziranga National Park, where visitors can often see more than 12 individuals together at one time.

24. Rhino horn is used in traditional Asian medicine. Powdered rhino horn is commonly used in traditional medicine. Some people will pay nearly £40,000 per kg for rhino horn, which is more than the current price for the same amount of gold. This leads to illegal hunting of rhinos for their horns, and is a major reason why some species are threatened with extinction.

25. Fighting rhinos. Black rhinos fight each other and have the highest rate of death for mammals in fights among the same species. 50% of males and 30% of females die from these intra-species fights.

Giant Hornless Rhinoceros-like Mammal (Extinct)

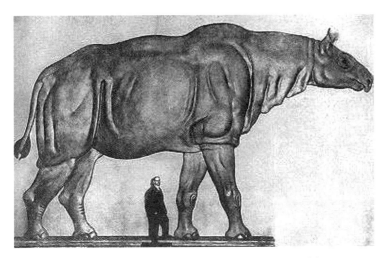

Paraceratherium was a gigantic, hornless, rhinoceros-like mammal, an ancestor of modern rhinoceroses.

It is the largest land mammal ever known to have existed and it lived in the forests of Central Asia between 23-34 million years ago.

Paraceratherium had a mobile upper lip, as well as long legs and a long neck, so that it could reach the leaves and twigs of the tall trees and large shrubs in the ancient forests.

The biggest fossils found show that it was approximately 4.8 m tall at the shoulders and 8 m in length from nose to rump. In the picture above, you can see how tall the animal was compared to a man.

Paraceratherium weighed about 16 tonnes. That's about the same weight as three African elephants put together!

Woolly Rhino (Extinct)

The woolly rhino first appeared about 350,000 years ago and may have survived until as recently as 10,000 years ago. They were hunted, possibly to extinction, by early humans; and they were painted on the walls of caves in France 30,000 years ago.

The woolly rhinoceros lived when ice and snow covered a lot of the land in the northern hemisphere. They had a thick fur coat and a layer of fat to keep them warm in the cold conditions.

The woolly rhino was a herbivore, with a flat-sided horn that allowed it to push away snow in order to graze on grass, shrubby sprouts, forbs, lichens, and mosses. Woolly rhinos had a broad front lip which helped them eat this type of food.

The range of the woolly rhino was from South Korea to Scotland to Spain. They may have had the largest range of any known rhinoceros, living or extinct. Their fossils have been discovered throughout Europe and Asia, especially in what is now Russia. Fossils of woolly rhinoceros horns show scratch marks that appear to have been caused by a 'to and fro' motion of the head as the animal pushed the snow away while searching for grass. Well-preserved remains have been discovered frozen in ice and buried in oil-saturated soils. At Staruni, in what is now the Ukraine, a complete carcass of a female woolly rhino was discovered buried in mud. The combination of oil and salt in the mud prevented the remains from decomposing, allowing the soft tissues to remain intact.

Woolly rhinos frequently inhabited the same areas as woolly mammoths. However they apparently never managed to move across the Bering Strait (Bering Land Bridge) and extend their range into North America. The woolly rhino lived just as their recent relatives do, alone or in very small family groups.

Sumatran Rhino (Asia)

The Sumatran rhino is the last surviving representative of the woolly rhino family.

Sumatran Rhino (continued)

Estimated number alive: 90-200

Current conservation status: Critically Endangered

Found in: Indonesia and northern Borneo (Malaysia)

Size: Sumatran rhinos are by far the smallest of the five species of rhinos, standing 1.20-1.45 m at the shoulder and weighing just 500-800 kg.

Skin and hair: Sumatran rhinos, sometimes called 'hairy rhinos', have grey leathery skin, which is covered with a coat of bristly, reddish-brown hair. Sumatran rhinos have hair because they are one of the most 'primitive' (oldest) rhinos; the closest relative of the extinct woolly rhinoceros.

Head: The head is 70-80 cm in length. Sumatran rhinos have two horns, dark grey to black in colour. Sumatran rhino horns are much smaller than those of the African species and the greater one-horned rhino; sometimes the horns just look like two raised bumps on the rhino's nose.

Lip: The upper lip of the Sumatran rhino is hooked and prehensile (which means 'able to grasp or hold something') so that it can browse on vegetation.

Teeth: Sumatran rhinos, unlike African rhinos, have long dagger-shaped lower incisor teeth. These teeth are very sharp and can cause deep wounds when used in fights.

Ears: Sumatran rhinos have a noticeable fringe of longer hairs around the outside of their ears

Speed: Sumatran rhinos can run fast and are very agile. They climb mountains easily and can negotiate very steep slopes and riverbanks. Walking through the dense rainforest is difficult for humans but Sumatran rhinos move through the forest very easily.

Tracks: Sumatran rhinos use a network of game trails that occur on ridges and along major rivers.

Habitat: The Sumatran rhino lives in dense tropical forest, both lowland and highland, and they spend a large part of the day wallowing in mud holes.

Food: Sumatran rhinos have lots of things to eat in the tropical rainforest and several hundred different rhino snacks have been recorded. They eat about 50-60 kg of plant matter every day. That's about 10% of their body weight.

Territory: Males have large territories (up to 50 km^2), which overlap with other males' territories. The females have much smaller ranges of about 10-15 km^2. They overlap with male territories, so that they have a chance to mate with several different males (which is good for genetic diversity).

Behaviour: Sumatran rhinos usually live alone. The exceptions are when male and female rhinos are courting and a female is with its calf. The Sumatran rhino is very vocal and communicates by using many different sounds, mostly whistling or whining.

Greater One-Horned 'Indian' Rhino (Asia)

Scientific name: *Rhinoceros unicornis*

Estimated number alive: 2,800-3,500

Current conservation status: Vulnerable

Found in: India and Nepal

Size: The greater one-horned rhino is the second-largest of all the rhinos. They weigh between 1,800-3,500 kg – that's as much as a transit van! They are 1.7-2.0 m tall at the shoulder, and 3.0-3.8 m long.

Skin: The skin of the greater one-horned rhino is very thick and forms heavy folds, which makes the rhino look as if it is wearing a suit of armour!

Lip: They have a prehensile upper lip, which helps them to grasp their food. Like black rhinos, they are browsers, and eat a wide mix of plants: fruit, leaves and branches of trees and shrubs, as well as the very tall elephant grass that covers much of their habitat and aquatic plants.

Head: Greater one-horned rhinos have just one horn.

This typically measures 20-30 cm long, and weighs around 1-2 kg. They use their horn to search for food and roots. They have long lower incisor teeth, which can grow up to 8 cm long in male rhinos. These teeth are used in fighting and can cause deep wounds.

Ears: Greater one-horned rhinos hear very well. They have hair around their ears to stop sand or dirt getting in.

Tail: Like the other rhino species, greater one-horned rhinos have tails, but they are usually stuck between the folds on the animal's two hind legs.

Speed: Greater one-horned rhinos can run fast – up to 40 km/h – and are very agile.

Tracks: Like all rhinos, they have three toes, with distinct toenails.

Habitat: Greater one-horned rhinos seem to love water! They are very good swimmers and can dive and feed under water. They also like wallowing in mud. The wet mud helps them to keep cool, and also keeps the flies from irritating their skin.

Territory: Males are territorial but only loosely define their land. The dominant males defend their territory from other males but let females move in and out of their territories as they like. The territories change according to food availability and with the regular monsoon flooding, when the shape of the river changes.

Behaviour: Greater one-horned rhinos are often solitary, except for females with small calves. However, if food is abundant, it is not unusual to see several animals all browsing close together. Greater one-horned rhinos use about twelve different sounds to communicate with each other, e.g. when a calf is looking for its mother, or a male is warning another male to keep out of its territory.

Lesser One-Horned 'Javan' Rhino (Asia)

Estimated number alive: 35-50

Current conservation status: Critically Endangered*

Found in: Indonesia

Size: Javan rhinos are similar in size to the African black rhino, but it is hard to say exactly how much they weigh, because only a few have actually been weighed. It it thought that most are between 900-1,800 kg. They are 1.4-1.8 m tall at the shoulder.

Lip: Javan rhinos have a long, pointed, and prehensile upper lip, which helps them to grasp their food.

Head: Javan rhinos are closely related to greater one-horned 'Indian' rhinos. They have the same heavy folds of skin, and they have just one horn, usually about 20 cm long. Male Javan rhino horns are generally longer than female rhino horns, which are often just a bump.

Ears: Javan rhinos hear very well, and have a good sense of smell, but are extremely short-sighted.

Speed: Javan rhinos have not been observed running but it is assumed that they are as good as Sumatran rhinos at moving through the forest.

Tracks: It is very, very unusual to see a Javan rhino. There are very few of them, they live in thick forest, and they are extremely shy. Only a small number of Javan rhinos have been exhibited in zoos. The last one in captivity died in 1907, in Adelaide Zoo, Australia. However, if walking through the jungle in Ujung Kulon National Park in Java, you may see Javan rhino dung or footprints, especially near waterholes and mud wallows.

Habitat: Javan rhinos used to live in lots of tropical landscapes but today the largest population remaining (about 30-35 individuals) lives in Ujung Kulon National Park in Java. They probably moved there from eastern Java as the land became settled by humans. Another smaller population, in Cat Tien national park in Vietnam, was confirmed as extinct in 2011.

Territory: Males in Ujung Kulon have territories of about 12-20 km^2 and overlap very little with other males. Territory is marked along the main trails by urine, dung, scrapes, and twisted saplings. Females in Ujung Kulon have smaller ranges, 3-14 km^2, and they overlap.

Behaviour: Javan, like Sumatran, rhinos are often solitary animals. The exceptions to this are when a female is raising her calf and when groups of Javan rhinos come together at the same mud-wallow or salt-licks. A salt-lick is a small hot spring, where water full of minerals seeps or bubbles out of the ground. Salt-licks are also known as 'mud volcanoes', because the mud bubbles and froths like a tiny volcano.

* The Javan rhino is the world's rarest land mammal.

Black Rhino (Africa)

Estimated number alive: 4,800-5,200

Current conservation status: Critically Endangered

Found in: Botswana, Kenya, Malawi, Namibia, Rwanda, South Africa, Swaziland, Tanzania, Zambia and Zimbabwe.

Size: Black rhinos stand on average about 1.5 m at the shoulder. They are very heavily built and can weigh anything between 800-1,800 kg – that's about as much as 20 men!

Lip: Black rhinos have a pointy, prehensile, upper lip. They are browsers, which means that they eat trees, shrubs, and herbs. Black rhinos use their special lip to pull twigs and branches into their mouths so they can bite them off. They need to eat more than 23 kg of food per day; and must also eat a variety of different plants to get all the nutrients they need.

Head: Because they feed on leaves and branches above the ground, black rhinos have a relatively short head and they tend to hold it up.

Ears: Black rhinos have very good hearing, which is

necessary as they spend most of their time in thick bush, where it is impossible to see very far. A black rhino's ears are large and rounded in shape so that they can catch the sounds around them. The ears can be turned to listen in different directions.

Speed: When a black rhino charges it can reach speeds of up to 45 km/h. This is much faster than most humans. They are also very agile and capable of turning sharp corners very quickly.

Tracks: The footprint of an adult black rhino is normally 20-25 cm across. The distance between steps (the 'stride'), as well as the size of the footprint, can help tell you how big the rhino is.

Habitat: Black rhinos can be found in many different habitats. They like to live in wooded areas, because they can find more food and shelter. However, some black rhinos have adapted to live in the deserts of Namibia.

Territory: Where there is a lot of food, like in parts of South Africa, territories may be as little as 2.6 km^2. If there is a shortage of food, like in the desert, one rhino may need as much as 133 km^2 to find enough to eat.

Behaviour: Black rhinos are thought to be bad-tempered and aggressive. Part of the reason for this is that, when people and black rhinos meet, it is often in the thick bush that black rhinos like to live in. The person and the rhino are both surprised when they meet each other. When a black rhino gets a surprise and a fright, its response is to give the person a fright back! They do this by charging. But black rhinos are like people, in that they have their own personalities. Some are friendly and curious, whilst others are grumpy and bad-tempered!

White Rhino (Africa)

Number alive: 20,000-21,000

Current conservation status: Near Threatened

Found in: Botswana, Kenya, Mozambique, Namibia, South Africa, Swaziland, Uganda, Zambia, Zimbabwe.

Size: White rhinos can be as tall as 1.8 m at the shoulder. They are very large and can weigh over 4,000 kg. White rhinos are the second largest land mammal in Africa (after elephants).

Lip: White rhinos are also known as 'square-lipped rhinos' because they have a square upper lip. They are grazers, which means that they eat grass. The lip is used to pluck grass. Having a very wide mouth helps the rhinos eat more. Such a large animal needs to eat a lot of food. White rhinos spend half their life eating.

Head: White rhinos have a relatively long head that helps make it easier for the animal to reach down to the grass they like to eat. They tend to hold their head low.

Ears: White rhino ears are narrower but longer than those of black rhinos. They are also more tube-shaped, rather than rounded.

Speed: When a white rhino charges, it can reach speeds of up to 40 km/h for a short distance. This is very fast for such a large animal.

Tracks: The front footprint of an adult white rhino is normally larger than that of black rhino.

Habitat: White rhinos live in the savannah, where there is plenty of grass for them to eat.

Territory: Territories vary in size from 2-5 km^2, depending on the availability of food. White rhinos are more territorial than black rhinos. A dominant male scents his territory by spraying urine. He will share this territory with one or two subordinate males and females. Generally, only the dominant male mates with the females, and he will try to keep breeding females inside his territory.

Behaviour: White rhinos are usually less aggressive than black rhinos. This is partly due to the different habitat they live in. In the savannah, where white rhinos live, it is easy to see them at a great distance, so the chances of getting too close to one, without it knowing, are very low. The more open country makes it easy for rhinos to see, hear, or smell people coming, and so there is plenty of time for them to move away if they wish. However, if you happen to be walking around in the African savannah, beware: white rhinos do sometimes charge!

QUIZ 2

About Rhinoceroses

This quiz is based on the 'FUN FACTS About Rhinoceroses' on pages 124-141. Answers at the back of the book. See www.jacktrelawny.com to print quizzes.

1) What is the scientific name for a greater one-horned 'Indian' rhinoceros ?
  A)   *Rhinoceros sondaicus*
  B)   *Dicerorhinus sumatrensis*
  C)   *Rhinoceros unicornis*
  D)   *Diceros bicornis*

2) How many toes do all rhinoceros have?
  A)   Three
  B)   Five
  C)   Two
  D)   Four

3) How many living species of rhinoceros are there?
  A)   Seven
  B)   Five
  C)   Six
  D)   Four

4) What does the Greek word 'rhinoceros' mean?
  A)   Thick skin
  B)   Nose horn
  C)   Long horn
  D)   Strong neck

5) Which living rhino species is related to the woolly rhino?

    A)   Javan rhino

    B)   Black rhino

    C)   Sumatran rhino

    D)   White rhino

6) Which is the world's rarest land mammal?

    A)   Javan rhino

    B)   Black rhino

    C)   Sumatran rhino

    D)   White rhino

7) What is rhino horn made from?

    A)   Keratin

    B)   Bone

    C)   Cartilage

    D)   Sinew

8) What is the length of the longest rhino horn measured?

    A)   125 cm

    B)   135 cm

    C)   145 cm

    D)   155 cm

9) What is the highest measured speed of a running rhino?

    A)   25 km/h

    B)   30 km/h

    C)   40 km/h

    D)   45 km/h

10) What is a group of rhinos called?

    A)   A flock

    B)   A crowd

    C)   A crash

    D)   A shoal

SAVE THE RHINO

Protection and Conservation

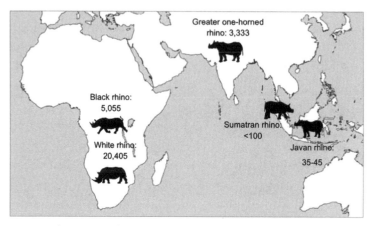

The map above and the text below are from
**www.savetherhino.org/rhino_info
/rhino_population_figures**

Save the Rhino International is a charity, co-founded, in 1994, by author Douglas Adams, who is perhaps best known for writing *A Hitchiker's Guide to the Galaxy*. He also wrote for the *Dr Who* television series.

In a BBC Radio 2 series called, *Last Chance to See*, broadcast in 1989, Douglas Adams, and zoologist, Mark Carwardine, set out to find endangered animals and make people more aware of the need to protect them.

Actor, Stephen Fry, a friend of Douglas Adams, also supports this charity and its aims. On 31 October 2010, Stephen and Mark Carwardine presented a special follow-up to the *Last Chance to See* radio series in a TV programme on BBC 2 called, *Return of the Rhino*.

The programme followed four of the last remaining northern white rhinos as they were transferred from Dvůr Králové Zoo in the Czech Republic to Ol Pejeta Conservancy, a protected reserve in Kenya, in a last-ditch attempt to save the subspecies from extinction.

At the beginning of the 20th century there were 500,000 rhinos across Africa and Asia. This number fell to 70,000 by 1970; and then further again to less than 30,000 in the wild today. Despite this bleak picture, and the continuing threat of poaching for their valuable horns, global rhino population figures have been increasing in recent years.

Large-scale poaching of the now critically endangered black rhino resulted in a dramatic 96% decline, from 65,000 individuals in 1970 to just 2,300 in 1993. Thanks to the persistent efforts of conservation programmes across Africa, black rhino numbers have risen since the early 1990s to a current population of about 5,000.

Save the Rhino supports many programmes protecting and conserving rhinos around the world.

The overwhelming rhino conservation success story is that of the southern white rhino in Africa. With numbers as low as 50 left in the wild in the early 1900s, the white rhino has now increased to over 20,000 and has become the most numerous of all the rhino species. The population is continuing to increase every year; however, there are concerns that the unprecedented rise in rhino poaching since 2008 may bring this species back into decline if the poaching is not reduced.

In Asia the populations of Sumatran and Javan rhinos are extremely low and both species are listed as critically endangered. There may be fewer than 100 Sumatran rhinos left in the wild, and efforts are now being invested in captive breeding in an attempt to boost the population.

History was made in June 2012 with the first Sumatran rhino calf ever to be born in captivity, at the Sumatran Rhino Sanctuary, in Indonesia.

The Javan story is sadly even more shocking with only an estimated 35 to 45 individuals left in Ujung Kulon National Park.

Save the Rhino are supporting local conservationists, who are working hard to increase the habitat for this species, since it is believed that the current habitat cannot support any more rhinos.

Rhino Protection Units have been set up to monitor and protect the remaining Javan and Sumatran rhinos.

If your family or school would like to help with these protection and conservation efforts, a good place to start is the Save the Rhino website:

www.savetherhino.org

GANDA'S JOURNEY

Map: Real vs Pretend

The map below shows both Ganda's real and pretend journeys by land, sea, and air.

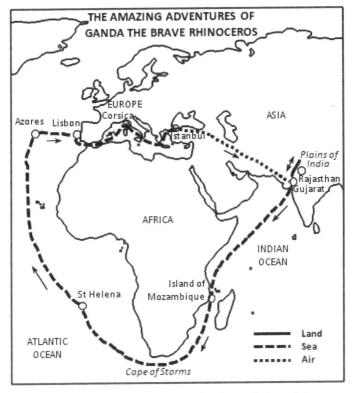

In the real history of Ganda's life, the mighty rhinoceros was taken from India to Portugal around the southern cape of Africa. In the pretend story that was inspired by the real history, I have changed and added elements to create the adventure. As you now know, in *The Emperor's Rhinoceros*, Ganda travels home on a flying carpet!

STORY DETECTIVES

'Finding Out' at the British Museum

The map of Ganda's Journey on page 147 shows how real history can be taken and changed to make a pretend story. Using real history and facts to make a pretend story is a genre of writing called 'historical fiction'.

The joint British Museum and BBC Radio 4 Podcast Project, *A History of the World in 100 Objects,* chose 13 of the objects or 'things' as specially for children. I have used each of these real 13 objects as inspiration for the *Thirteen Things* series of adventure stories.

To write historical fiction, or any other type of story, I like to do a lot of research to get ideas. When I visit schools, I tell children that *half* my job is 'finding out'. Half the time, I'm a 'Story Detective'. If I constantly find things out, I'll always have something to write about.

On 22 May 2014, I visited the British Museum in London to find out as much as I could about the 13 objects that have inspired this new series of stories. There were lots of other 'story detectives' at the museum; children who were finding things out with their school teachers (please visit our website – link below – to view pictures).

Luckily, my wife and my mum (who had travelled up from Cornwall to see us) were keen to come with me. My mum, who is now retired, was a primary school teacher for many years and my wife has two degrees; which means they're very good people to help me find out things so that I can write my stories!

We started with the Rosetta Stone object or 'thing'. It's one of the most popular exhibits with visitors to the museum. The Royal Game of Ur was one of my favourite things. When I found out it was 5,000 years old and that children played the game with dice and counters, it really made me think that people all that time ago were very much like us today. There are even squares on the board where you are 'safe' and can throw the dice again, which is just like some of our modern board games. Another of my favourite 'things' was the Sutton Hoo helmet. It is just like the helmet described in one of my favourite ancient stories: *Beowulf.* There is a dragon-type creature in the Beowulf story; can you spot the dragon hidden in the helmet design? Clue: the eyebrows are also wings.

I bought a postcard with a picture of 'Durer's Rhinoceros' on the front as a momento of the object that has inspired the first story in the *Thirteen Things* series: *The Emperor's Rhinoceros.*

I recommend a British Museum visit to everyone who can get there. Entry is free. Since its work is so important, your school or family may like to consider giving directly or perhaps organising a fund-raising project for making a donation to the museum to help with display, care, and preservation of the collection.

The British Museum is a huge place. If you're going to visit, my suggestion would be to make a plan in advance. The 13 objects took a few hours to locate and view. Some were on loan to other exhibitions.

There are details of all the exhibition rooms and current status of exhibits on the British Museum website, so that's a good place to start a plan for a visit:

www.britishmuseum.org

To see pictures from this and more Story Detective articles, go to this link:

www.jacktrelawny.com/story-detective

JACK TRELAWNY

School Author Visitor

Jack Trelawny first became known as a school author when he wrote six books in the *Kernowland in Erthwurld* series and began visiting schools.

Jack's second series, *Thirteen Things*, is inspired by 13 objects from the joint British Museum and BBC radio podcast project: *A History of the World in 100 Objects*.

100 Objects

When the British Museum and BBC had completed their joint project, they specially chose thirteen of the objects for children.

13 Objects = *13 Things*

As a children's author and regular school visitor, Jack Trelawny is discovering the true stories of the 13 objects, and using each of them as inspiration for his historical fiction adventures in the new *Thirteen Things* series.

Thirteen Things 1

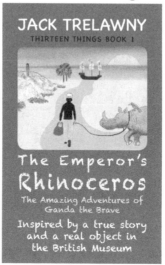

The Emperor's Rhinoceros, the first book in the *Thirteen Things* series, is inspired by Dürer's Rhinoceros, Object 75 in the joint British Musuem / BBC project.

Dürer's Rhinoceros

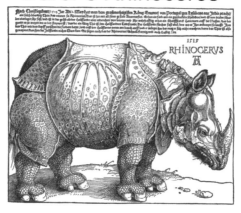

Holt Farm Junior School
at the British Museum
after Jack Trelawny's author visit

The British Museum and BBC have provided websites, museum tours, and other free resources for each of the thirteen objects.

Holt Farm Junior School at the British Museum
Photography by pupil, Leon T.

Children enjoy using these resources to discover more about the *Thirteen Things* after being introduced to them by Jack's stories. See the following pages for more about the British Museum and BBC resources for children.

Note: From Autumn Term 2014, this teaching format - of using museum objects to bring history to life - will be part of the new curriculum in many UK schools.

BBC Primary History: World History Resources

The BBC children's website can be used as a free resource by teachers and parents for all thirteen of the objects in Jack Trelawny's *Thirteen Things* series.

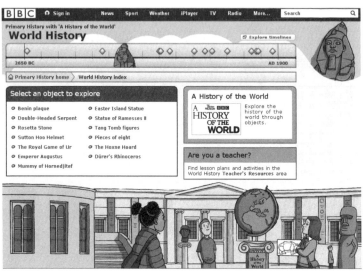

BBC Primary History World History website

13 Objects = *13 Things*	
- Benin Plaque	- Easter Island Statue
- Double-Headed Serpent	- Statue of Ramesses II
- Rosetta Stone	- Tang Tomb Figures
- Sutton Hoo Helmet	- Pieces of Eight
- The Royal Game of Ur	- The Hoxne Hoard
- Emperor Augustus	- Dürer's Rhinoceros
- Mummy of Hornedjitef	

There are quizzes, lesson plans, and activities on the site. For these and more children's resources at the BBC, see:

www.bbc.co.uk/schools/primaryhistory/worldhistory

British Musuem:
Learn World History
with Objects or 'Things'

The British Museum has provided a website and offers free activity trails. These resources can be used by teachers and parents for all 13 of the objects in the *Thirteen Things* series.

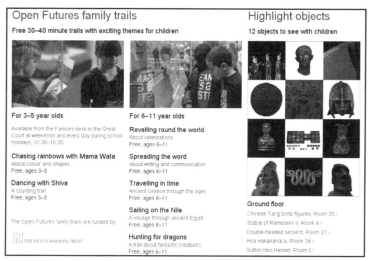

British Museum website

NOTE: At various times, some objects are preserved in storage or loaned to other exhibitions around the world. This means that sometimes not all the 13 things/objects will be exhibited in the children's activity trail.

For these and more children's resources at the British Museum, see:

**www.britishmuseum.org/visiting/family_visits/
13_objects_for_children.aspx**

**www.britishmuseum.org/visiting/family_visits/
activity_trails.aspx**

A History of the World in 100 Objects

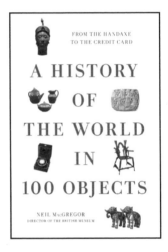

For adults interested in all 100 objects, there is a wonderful illustrated book by the Director of the British Museum, Neil MacGregor.

The book is described by the publisher as follows: 'Neil MacGregor's *A History of the World in 100 Objects* takes a bold, original approach to human history, exploring past civilizations through the objects that defined them. Encompassing a grand sweep of human history, *A History of the World in 100 Objects* begins with one of the earliest surviving objects made by human hands, a chopping tool from the Olduvai Gorge in Africa, and ends with objects which characterise the world we live in today.'

Adults can listen to the free podcasts and learn more by starting at the following links:

www.bbc.co.uk/ahistoryoftheworld

www.britishmuseum.org/ahistoryoftheworld

Jack Trelawny School Author Visits: Assemblies, Skype, and Workshops

Jack makes FREE visits to schools with his 'Edutainment' Shows, which combine 'education with entertainment' and 'learning with fun'.

At the time of writing, July 2014, he has visited more than 1,200 schools and presented his books and story-making ideas to over 250,000 children in the UK.

Left:
Presenting the 'Edutainment' Show

Below:
Book-signing event after the show

Jack also conducts UK and international Skype visits for schools, during which he talks about stories and writing to children around the world via the internet.

For class workshops, Jack visits schools with his *Story House*, a simple, step-by-step, creative writing system that helps children build their own stories using the expandable Story House template and links from across the curriculum; as well as the widest possible range of other resources, such as the BBC and British Museum.

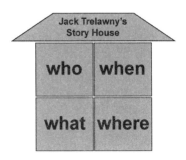

The 'house' starts simply for younger children. It then builds into a complete system which older children can use to create their own new stories and to break down existing stories into understandable parts.

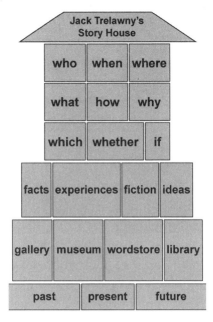

Arranging and Booking
School Author Visits

Teachers can find out more about Jack Trelawny's FREE School Author Visits and fee-based Story House Creative Writing Workshops on the 'Schools' page of his website:

www.jacktrelawny.com/schools

For more information
or to book a school visit, contact:
Jane Bennett, Events Manager,
Campion Books (Publishers):

info@campionpublishing.com

QUIZ ANSWERS

Quiz 1: *The Emperor's Rhinoceros*
Answers to Quiz 1 questions on pages 122-123:

1)	**D**	**India**
2)	**B**	**One**
3)	**C**	**Elephant**
4)	**A**	**Rajasthan**
5)	**C**	**120 days**
6)	**D**	**King Manuel**
7)	**A**	**Dhow**
8)	**D**	**Istanbul**
9)	**C**	**Four**
10)	**B**	**Three**

Quiz 2: About Rhinoceroces
Answers to Quiz 2 questions on pages 142-143:

1)	**C**	***Rhinoceros unicornis***
2)	**A**	**Three**
3)	**B**	**Five**
4)	**B**	**Nose horn**
5)	**C**	**Sumatran rhino**
6)	**A**	**Javan rhino**
7)	**A**	**Keratin**
8)	**C**	**145 cm**
9)	**D**	**45 km/h**
10)	**C**	**A crash**

To print these and other quizzes, go to:
www.jacktrelawny.com